Her baton seemed to glow, tracing a lighted path through the air. Afterglow lines showed where the baton had been, and she had never felt such an acute awareness of the concentration of the other performers on her, how their energy was directed at her, through her, and out of her again. When the music paused she could feel the music to come seething to escape.

And it escaped—she was conducting music, conducting electricity, conducting light. Her intensity, instead of collapsing inward like a black hole, exploded outward—a nova that sang through her fingertips and haloed the choir and musicians. Her entire body was caught up in the magic; she rose to her tiptoes again and again, reaching higher in an agony of ecstasy . . .

The cathedral was utterly silent—then the sounds of hundreds of people breathing in slowly, as if waking from deep sleep, filled Nick's ears and she realized she had not heard the music, only felt it.

Finally, after what seemed like an endless stream of people, one particular pair of blue eyes shone at her, and Nick saw the trace of tears on Carolyn's face. She moved closer to Carolyn.

"What is it?" She traced a line of the tears with her thumb.

Carolyn, moving it seemed to Nick in slow motion, put her hand on Nick's cheek. "Yes, you're real," she said. "Nick—it was magic. Magic," she repeated. "I can't find the words . . ."

WRITING AS KARIN KALLMAKER:

One Degree of Separation
Maybe Next Time
Substitute for Love
Frosting on the Cake
Unforgettable
Watermark
Making Up for Lost Time
Embrace in Motion
Wild Things
Painted Moon
Car Pool
Paperback Romance
Touchwood
In Every Port
Sugar

WRITING FOR BELLA AFTER DARK:

All the Wrong Places
Once Upon a Dyke: New Exploits of Fairy Tale Lesbians

WRITING AS LAURA ADAMS:

Christabel

The Tunnel of Light Trilogy:
Sleight of Hand
Seeds of Fire

Daughters of Pallas:
Night Vision
The Dawning

Paperback Romance

Karin Kallmaker

Bella
BOOKS

2005

Bella Books, Inc.
P.O. Box 10543
Tallahassee, FL 32302

First published 1992 by Naiad Press

Printed in the United States of America on acid-free paper
First Edition

Editor: Christi Cassidy
Cover designer: Sandy Knowles

ISBN 1-59493-033-3

*For my Woman of Cups
and in memory of Carolyn Hadley*

The Third is for Turning On

Acknowledgments

My gratitude to all the women who have done what they had to do, without thinking, without hesitation, so that I could stand on a street corner and kiss my lover without thinking, without hesitation.

1

Overture

Carolyn was going to be tickled lavender. Alison smiled at her own fancy — Carolyn would only be tickled pink. Alison was dreaming about the lavender part.

Luscious lavender or merely pink — it didn't matter, she told herself, as long as she was able to deliver the check in person. Waiting was excruciating. To pass the time she called out, "Any sign of Federal Express?"

Devon's voice floated back to her, edged with impatience. "Not yet." Unsaid, but hanging in the air was the added message, "For the tenth time in the last ten minutes."

Alison sighed. The check absolutely, positively had to be here by ten o'clock if she was going to deliver it herself, otherwise it would have to go by messenger. *And I'll miss the expression on her face, and the hug of thanks. Maybe two hugs.*

A part of Alison — the part she listened to least — told her she should not rearrange her life around the possibility of a hug from Carolyn. But what the heck — she'd suffered from unrequited love for so long it was a fixture in her life.

She tried to concentrate on the contract she was going to negotiate in Los Angeles this afternoon. It was her first contract negotiation with Pullman & Sons, and the author involved deserved as much attention as Alison was presently giving to Carolyn. Carolyn was of course Alison's favorite author, but she had to take a back seat to the business at hand or McNamara Literary would become a one-client agency — a situation too precarious for Alison's peace of mind. Fortified by the specter of negative cash flow, Alison set herself to unraveling Article VI, Section A, Part 34(f).

The front door of her tiny office suite opened sometime later and Alison realized with a shock that it was almost eleven. Even as she leapt past Devon and snatched the proffered envelope from the courier, Alison silently wailed that today of all days the guaranteed ten o'clock delivery time had not been met. *You'd think Sacramento was Barstow or Bakersfield or, God forbid, Fresno.*

Back at her desk, she zipped the strip on the package and shook out the contents. She didn't give the signed contract a second glance. She knew by heart every detail of the arrangement for Carolyn's — or rather, Carly Vincent's — first three romances to be distributed in Canadian and Australian supermarkets and bookstores. It was the check that gained all her attention.

"Can I touch it?" Devon leaned over Alison's shoulder.

"You may look," Alison said. She held it out for his perusal.

Devon whistled. "Looks like I'm due for a bonus," he said with his usual lack of humility. "And if she doesn't get the hots for you after this, then she never will."

"Keep it up and there's no bonus," Alison said crushingly.

"Okay. I'll say no more. So I'm definitely getting a bonus. That's nice." Devon smiled serenely at Alison.

"Con artist," she said fondly, then she grimaced as she remembered the time. "I'm off to the bank."

As she hurried up the street, Alison could only think about what Carolyn's portion would mean to Carolyn. It had been at least nine months since Carolyn had returned from Paris. She'd gone to do research, to give Carly Vincent an international flair. Alison's upper lip took on a Billy Idol curl as she recalled the completely inappropriate turn Carolyn's research had taken. First had come the ecstatic telegram, "Got married you'll love him. Home soon." Alison's world had rocked; she doubted she would "love him." Matters hardly improved when two weeks later a second telegram arrived: "Single again. Will explain when home."

Alison had remained Carolyn's friend over the years, their ties to each other remaining strong even when Alison spent several years in New York. Though not aware of how or where Carolyn spent every night, Alison had suspected that Carolyn had never had any kind of meaningful sexual experience. That fact kept Alison hoping more and more intensely over the years that some day Carolyn would realize Alison could be there for her in more ways than just as an agent and friend. It had still been a shock to find out, while Carolyn sobbed out a garbled account of the entire fiasco, that Carolyn had indeed, like the heroines in her novels, gone to her marriage bed a virgin. Carolyn had said bitterly that she didn't know what she'd waited thirty years for.

What could I have done? There hadn't been anything to do but listen and soothe. Carolyn had been shattered — her romantic, storybook marriage had ended with her new husband's infidelity, a convenient annulment and intervention by the American Consulate. Alison suspected once the romance had worn off, shortly into the wedding night, Carolyn had not been able to respond sexually to her hero. But Carolyn, pouring the sad story into Alison's receptive shoulder, believed she was frigid and that the entire mess was her fault.

After that, Carolyn's emotions had iced over and had yet to thaw. Before the marriage she and Carolyn regularly got together just to split a Sara Lee cheesecake and watch old movies. Since the marriage, it was business and business only that brought them together. Carolyn dodged discussions of anything except work. The entire affair had altered the foundation of their long-standing friendship, but on the bright side — if there was a bright side — Carolyn had finally come to the conclusion that she was not sexually compatible with men. This was good news for Alison. The bad news was that Carolyn had decided she wasn't sexually compatible with anyone. Alison had taken Carolyn's lead — and she'd been waiting for nine long months for an offer to do anything together that didn't involve business.

She was in luck at the bank, although the speediest teller in the world wouldn't give her the half hour she needed to get to Carolyn's and then to the airport. The bank teller, Alison's favorite for reasons other than efficiency, completed the transactions quickly and with a smile that was a little more intimate than the job required. One of these days Alison was going to follow up on the invitation the teller had been discretely extending to her ever since they'd seen each other at the Sacramento Pride Faire. Maybe this one could cure her addiction to Carolyn Vincense.

Back at her desk, Alison swept the contract file into her briefcase and confirmed that she did indeed have her plane tickets. She checked her watch again, but time had not stopped. If only Carolyn didn't live all the way out in the 'burbs — it was a twenty-five minute struggle up J Street, over the American River and then on up Fair Oaks Boulevard, just seven miles or so, on surface streets. By the time she drove to Carolyn's, hugged her (with intense savoring) and then drove to the airport, she'd miss her flight by a good half an hour. Sacramento was getting more like Los Angeles every day.

She considered holding onto the cashier's check until tomorrow evening, but Alison-the-prudent-agent knew that such a large chunk of money shouldn't be sitting around not earning interest. Since she wouldn't be back in town until tomorrow evening, she resigned herself to giving Carolyn's check into Devon's safekeeping with strict instructions to messenger it immediately. Alison-the-unrequited-lover was quite depressed.

When her plane was finally airborne, she closed her eyes and imagined the ice around Carolyn melting at last, imagined Carolyn reaching for Alison's embrace in gratitude.

Her fantasies did not stop at a mere embrace. They never did.

2
Prelude du Oblivious

"Why don't you take a long trip or something? Maybe you'll get over being blocked."

"I'm not blocked, I'm just taking a break," Carolyn protested with as much conviction as she could muster. Terminal goose bumps broke out over the uncovered parts of her body — which was most of her. She was in the kitchen; she wished she had a longer cord on the phone so she could stand on the carpet. She was not about to tell Margot she had still been in bed. "I've just been trying out some new themes. Thinking about other things." Like the nature of time and space and why anyone would want to eat frozen Twinkies. Deep, complicated thoughts that had nothing whatsoever to do with romance or sex.

"If you say so, honey," Margot said. "It just seems to me that —"

"Tell me about the plans for Curt's party," Carolyn broke in. She loved her sister-in-law dearly, but she just couldn't bear to have Margot explain one more time that love was like riding a bicycle. Margot should talk. Curt had been her first love and eight years later, he hadn't given Margot any regrets Carolyn knew of.

"— Doesn't it sound like fun? You did keep tomorrow night free, didn't you?" Margot finished.

Carolyn realized she hadn't heard a word and that she couldn't feel her toes. "Yeah, I'll be there," she promised. "Give the two munchkins an Auntie Carl hug."

Carolyn hurried back to the bedroom where she thrust her frozen feet into mismatched old, thick socks and pulled yesterday's sweatshirt — I ♥ Sacramento — over her head. All her sweatpants were dirty, so she rummaged in the laundry basket for the least dirty pair and pulled them on. She promised herself she'd start a load of laundry sometime soon. It wasn't as if anyone would be around to catch her in this disreputable state.

She warmed her face over boiling ramen noodles while she gulped her first cup of Morning Thunder tea. Mama, she thought, I know this is a rotten meal, but I'll get back on the right track soon. She

8

wondered if her parents were watching her from some heavenly perch, shaking their heads over the rise and fall of their once-independent daughter.

After breakfast/lunch was accomplished without the actual intake of nutrition, she knew it was time to go to work. If she got some work done at least she wouldn't be lying to Alison about it anymore. All Alison wanted to know about lately was work, work, work. As Carolyn forced herself to her study, she wondered when she would stop feeling as if she were on her way to an all-day calculus exam without a pencil and without having taken the class.

One long greenhouse window, filled with ferns and African violets and a dozen other plants in declining stages of health, stretched along the outer wall. The opposite wall was lined with sturdy bookshelves which housed everything from Dickens to Danielle Steele. One shelf she reserved for the collected writings of Carly Vincent. There were five paperbacks there already and room for many more.

Carly Vincent, Carolyn thought, has just one little problem: Carly's inspiration was like a can of warm soda gone flat.

She'd done everything she could think of. She'd turned the computer away from the window three months ago but now she just swiveled the chair around to look out at the garden and its hint of new greens. The white and purple-streaked crocuses had already started to fade. Some days she would stare for hours, thinking about going back to school for her doctorate. Except she was pretty sure you couldn't get an undeclared doctorate. She didn't feel up to making declarations.

She'd tried rereading her favorite romances to get

the right mindset but every time the hero growled or the heroine swooned Carolyn either burst into laughter or felt vaguely sick. Romance no longer gave her a thrill on any level, and so Carly Vincent had nothing to write about. Carolyn was now at a stage where she felt that if she left her writing alone long enough a new twist might occur to her — something she could believe in again.

In the meantime, this room was the only one in the house that was spotless because she had spent hours cleaning instead of writing. There was a fresh piece of paper in the printer which was waiting patiently for something to print. Yesterday it had printed the grocery list (item three had been laundry detergent) but she hadn't felt up to going to the store.

She slid into her ergonomic chair, turned on her computer, adjusted her screen height and the desk lamp, then clicked into her document for her untitled outline. She set the margins just so, again, and made sure the typeface was her preferred serif, again. Her fingertips poised to start the outline, list the settings, make bios of the characters, but she was hypnotized by the bright March sun as it streamed through the window at her back. Then she noticed how dirty the windows were.

She spent the rest of the morning washing all the windows, inside and out, and then she thoroughly dusted all of the mini-blinds in the entire house, just for good measure. The sun no longer streamed in, it poured in, forming huge pools of gold that illuminated every threadbare spot in the carpets and every dust bunny lurking in the corners.

Carolyn sighed. How on earth did a piece of Kleenex get tracked into the entry way?

After a snack of cereal — during which she had the revelation that her cereal tasted like the box it came out of — she sorted a bag of M&Ms by color. She ate the orange ones first, since they were the least plentiful, then quickly polished off tan, green, red, yellow and dark brown. She told herself to call Alison and make arrangements to meet at the gym before it was too late for her thighs.

M&Ms devoured, she considered getting a soda, but then decided she must do *something* on the book. At least she could choose names. Her heroine was going to be Della, but in Alison's draft the heroine would be Heather, which would nauseate Alison. Carolyn saw the reflection of her wicked smile in the computer screen.

She still needed to name the hero. Fingers poised, she mulled over a name to go with Della — well, Perry or Mason was obvious. "Perry. Mason. Remington. Steele. Hamilton. Burger. Blake. Carrington. Egbert. ø*¢§a°r¥æ!" She mashed her fingers on the keyboard and watched the gibberish march across the screen. It looked just like her state of mind.

She deleted the line, and then thought the name might come to her if she developed some character traits. "Okay, Carly. You see him standing across the room — he's everything you could want in a man." She fought down a mental gag at the idea of finding a man attractive ever again, and then typed, "Intriguing. Tall. Imposing. Dark. Arrogant. Imperious. Impotent." Sigh.

She deleted the line, then picked up a paper clip and slowly unbent it. If she couldn't come up with a hero there was no point in writing anything else. But the problem with creating the perfect hero was that she no longer believed a real model for the perfect hero existed. It would be more accurate if she were to pattern her hero after the men at her gym. Self-centered. Egotistical. Closet chauvinists. When they thought no "Babes" were nearby they talked about how they couldn't drink coffee at night anymore, which beer had the best commercials and how mean their women bosses were — hey, check out the Babe on the bicycle. They tended to talk freely around Carolyn, so she guessed she wasn't in the Babe category. What was so funny was that they would shut up and flex when Alison was around and Alison never gave them a second glance — she was devoted to her work.

Once, just once, Carolyn told herself, I'd like to write a story about someone with a passion, preferably for something that wasn't illegal, misogynistic, or that involved beer morning, noon and night. Her own true life experience had left her imagination with as much voltage as mashed potatoes.

Her dull, reliable — okay, kind of sweet and nice — brother had recently suggested that Carolyn use her experience in Paris as the basis for her next romance, except give the Unfortunate Affair (his usual phrase *du jour* about the entire mess) a happy ending. It worked, up to a point. Girl goes on once-in-a-lifetime vacation to Paris. Girl meets Boy. Boy and Girl see the romantic sights of Paris together. Boy proposes to Girl. Girl accepts. Roses, a

Parisian chapel, a stop at the American Consulate and Boy and Girl get Married. Quite a storybook affair. A real paperback romance.

Except that Girl finds great disappointment on wedding night. Wonders what on earth she had saved herself for. But Girl tries to please. Boy aware of Girl trying. Boy reestablishes masculinity elsewhere. Girl and Boy agree to annulment. A few lies to the right officials and Boy and Girl are no longer married.

It wasn't any easier for Girl that it had only been a holiday romance, and that after it was over she hardly felt touched. In fact, Girl felt downright numb.

And Girl had no hero, no book, no nothing. The grocery shelves from Plymouth, CA to Plymouth, MA were going to miss Carly Vincent's annual contribution. But nothing had sparked her imagination. Carly couldn't create the kind of character she wanted to fall in love with because Carolyn didn't want to fall in love again. She had tried it once and it looked like it would cost her her livelihood.

She told herself it wouldn't kill her to get a real job. She'd known this Carly Vincent business wouldn't last. It was too easy.

The doorbell rang, jolting Carolyn from her train of thought just before it started down an extremely depressing track. She signed for the envelope — it was probably some document to sign that Alison was in a tizzy about having. She'd look at it later. Carolyn went to get a soda and decided to finish off the Cheetos, even though she'd been saving them for a special occasion.

13

Back at the word processor she stared at the empty screen. *Girl meets Boy. Boy meets Girl.* She set her fingers on the keyboard again. It was all supposed to work out. It was supposed to be perfect and normal and perfectly normal. Carolyn raised her hands. Her fingers were trembling. Maybe Curt was right. If she wrote it down she might make some sense of what had happened to her in Paris. She might make some use of it after all. She took a deep breath and let her fingers fly.

She kept her eyes closed most of the time and just typed. Every detail, every image, every thought, every question — she didn't stop to read any of it, she just let it pour out. She felt darkness inside draining away.

It was after sunset when the phone rang. Carolyn realized, as she staggered to the phone, that her body was cramped and her senses dazed.

"So, what did you think when you opened it?" Alison's voice had a faraway sound to it.

"Opened what?"

"It didn't get there? Devon is dead meat —"

"Wait, wait, wait," Carolyn interrupted. "Are you talking about the thing that arrived by messenger?" Carolyn couldn't believe she had forgotten about it. Where was it?

"What else would I be talking about? Christ, Carolyn, you scared me — you didn't open it?" Alison sounded a bit upset.

"Sorry, I was working," Carolyn said. "I'll get it." She looked frantically around the kitchen. "I had it when I got a Coke," she said, thinking out loud.

"You lost it?" There was a long pause. Then

Alison said, in a high, faint voice, "Please don't tell me you lost it."

"No, it's here somewhere." Carolyn set the phone down. She could hear Alison's voice echoing shrilly against the Formica. She mentally backtracked, then triumphantly opened the refrigerator. The envelope was on the egg carton, which she noticed was empty. "I have it right here," she told Alison. "Where are you, anyway?" She slit the envelope and opened it.

"El Lay," Alison said. "Otherwise I'd have delivered it in person. Carolyn? Carolyn?"

"This is an April Fool's joke, isn't it?" Carolyn swallowed once. It had to be a fake. "This is just an incredible simulation, isn't it? I can't actually cash this, can I?" Carolyn clutched the phone to her ear.

"I wanted to surprise you," Alison said. Her voice, now at its normal husky cadence, conveyed an ear-to-ear smile across hundreds of miles of fiber-optic phone lines. "I earned every penny of my share."

"Alison!" Carolyn gave the check a quick glance, thinking if she looked too long one of the zeros might fall off. "You didn't even give me a hint."

"I wasn't sure the deal was ever going to jell. In the end it took so long I figured it was merciful you didn't know you were going to sizzle in Canada and Down Under," Alison said.

"Didn't you need my signature or anything?"

Alison sighed. "You'll never understand our contract, will you? Between me and your publisher we control more of Carly Vincent than you do. You are so lucky I'm not a crook."

Carolyn began to picture a soft green carpet the

color of a mossy forest floor. And curtains bringing warm peaches and cream into the most icy Sacramento winter night. And tinted dual pane windows to keep out the most scorching Sacramento summer day. And a parquet floor, new shingles, and a great big bathtub – there were a hundred decadent luxuries her parents had forgone in favor of sending their children to college. Some decorating changes would make it her house at last. And –

"Hel-lo Carolyn! Hey — remember me, calling long distance?"

"Sorry, I was spending the money in my mind."

"I want you to do something other than buy new carpets and roof the house with that money."

"How do you always know what I'm thinking?"

Alison's low laugh flowed through the phone. "I know you inside out. Do something exotic. Brush up on all those languages you've let rust to pieces. I hear carpeting and plumbing running around your head. Wouldn't the South Seas be far more satisfactory than new pipes?"

"I just might consider it — I feel so on top of the world. Thank you, Alison, you are a terrific agent! Of course you're the only agent I've ever had, but I know you're terrific."

"You're at liberty to include that information in your next book."

"But I *am* going to redecorate. Do you know anyone good?" Alison always knew somebody.

Alison hesitated, then said, "Yeah, umm, Samantha Beckwith — I've heard nothing but good things about her work. She's in the book."

"I'll call her."

"Well, if you decide to take a trip or something,

I'll see that the lawn gets watered. It's the least the best agent in the world can do for you."

"You're not a bad friend either," Carolyn said.

"Then take me to dinner some time soon." Alison's voice was softer, less husky.

"Okay, it's a date."

After a completely indulgent trip to the grocery store, where she bought not one but *two* types of muffins and a supply of hand-dipped ice cream bars, Carolyn called her brother. Curt reminded her that she'd promised to start a retirement plan as soon as she had some money.

"The money'll be safe, won't it?" Carolyn nibbled on a muffin.

"Of course," he said. "I'll split it between tax-exempt municipal bonds and government-insured stuff. A nice, steady return, and you'll get some tax breaks."

"Okay, but I want to start small," Carolyn said. The words *tax-exempt* made her sleepy.

"You sound just like Mom and Dad. I'll bring the prospectuses and forms home from work. Come over early before the party tomorrow and I'll tell you more about it." Curt's voice became less official-investment-officerish. "I hope you're going to do something to the house, though. I mean, you don't have to if you don't want to, but I wouldn't mind if you did, you know. It's your house now."

"Well, I was thinking about some serious redecorating," Carolyn admitted. She hadn't known how Curt would feel about it.

"Good! The place looks so much like it did when we were kids, I expect Mom or Dad to walk in."

"I know. It happens to me from time to time."

"So make it your house."

Carolyn felt relieved. He concluded the call with a reminder about her tax obligations. Ouch. She got out the forms that Rochelle — Alison's tax wizard — had prepared so Carolyn could calculate her quarterly deposits. She winced at the final number. Her new, higher payment was due in just a few weeks. But even allowing for a pretty swell trip somewhere, there was certainly enough left for a new roof and new carpeting and finishing the installation of mini-blinds in the rest of the house, and maybe some new furniture. The house needed a breath of fresh air just as much as she herself did.

The next morning she set up an appointment with Samantha Beckwith. At the mention of Alison's name, Samantha eagerly offered to stop by the following day. Nothing was too good for a friend of Alison's.

When Carolyn opened the door to Samantha, she was immediately intimidated. Samantha looked nothing like her cheery and informal voice — she appeared every inch the type who lived for frozen whites and icy blues and merciless mirrored walls. Samantha herself was a tall, regal queen — a six-foot Whitney Houston-slim figure with masses of black hair swept into a perfect chignon and fastened with two long rhinestone-tipped hat pins. Carolyn felt mousey and pasty, like a plant grown in a closet. She took comfort in the fact that she was wearing *clean* sweatpants and that it was possible to read the "Make Pizza, Not War" emblazoned on her sweatshirt.

"I — I don't want to get rid of any of my things," she explained as she escorted Samantha to the living room. "I would hate it if my reading stack looked – out of place." She waved a hand at the comfortable clutter, and noticed for the first time that the reading stack had become a furnishing in itself.

Samantha smiled and the regal demeanor vanished. "It will be a welcome change," she said. "I'm tired of designing hermetically sealed show places. You want to l-i-v-e here."

It took Carolyn a second to form in her mind the word Samantha had spelled out. Then she smiled, suddenly at ease. "You understand," she said. She felt a wave of relief.

"It's one of my better qualities. Let's identify your preferences for c-o-l-o-r, and then we'll decide how to get those colors into your h-o-m-e," Samantha said with a conspiratorial grin. The way she spelled out her words reminded Carolyn of a spelling bee, but the overall effect was fun. Everybody Alison knew seemed to be a lot of fun. Carolyn sat down before one of the thick swatch books Samantha hoisted easily onto the table. As Carolyn turned to the orange and peach shades something tickled her ear. She turned her head slightly and was temporarily mesmerized by a long, wavy strand of silky, black hair that had escaped from the chignon.

"Sorry," Samantha said. "It's always coming down." Carolyn watched as Samantha pulled out the pins and ruffled her hair. "These things were rubbing my scalp all day." The ebony masses tumbled down and settled elegantly along Samantha's shoulders and back.

"Uh – why do you wear it that way?" It looked incredibly soft — just like a shampoo advertisement but real.

"My designer persona. If my softball buddies saw me they'd have a h-o-o-t."

"It's hard to picture you in a softball jersey." But somehow on Carolyn's mental sketchpad there appeared a perfect rendition of Samantha jumping for a fly ball.

"I love it. Alison and I are on the same team."

Carolyn hadn't known that Alison played softball. It sounded like fun, actually. Maybe she'd look into joining up.

"I see you're partial to peach. That Mango Ruby is spectacular but I still haven't been able to come up with a good coordinating shade. What about textures?"

It was an hour and a half before they were decided on fabrics and blinds and several patterns of wallcoverings. Carolyn trailed behind Samantha for another thirty minutes while she measured walls and windows. Samantha moved economically, measuring and making notes with great efficiency.

"Well, that's it." Samantha let her tape measure coil in with a snap.

The snap broke Carolyn out of her reverie of watching Samantha move gracefully around the house. Alison seemed to know so many competent women: Rochelle the tax wizard, Paulette the plumber, Peggy the computer repair expert, Linda the masterful travel agent and now Samantha. "Sorry, I was daydreaming." Carolyn led the way toward the front door to hide an inexplicable blush. "Well, thanks for, umm, stopping by so quickly."

"My pleasure," Samantha said, effortlessly scooping up the thick books of swatches and wallcoverings.

"Like I said, I might be taking a trip soon, but if I do, I'll let you know. I think Alison would act as my stand-in."

Samantha smiled broadly. "I wouldn't mind working with Alison at all. Not at all. Just let me know."

Samantha's smile left Carolyn feeling slightly dazzled but confused — had she missed a joke? She felt herself flush again, but Samantha waved a casual goodbye, apparently not noticing anything odd.

After the strange flush had completely faded, Carolyn called Alison, who answered with her usual slightly breathy hello.

"I'm getting redecorated," Carolyn said.

"Oh, so you did call Sam. How'd you get along?"

"Great. She knows just what I want."

"It's her g-i-f-t," Alison said with a laugh. Carolyn explained that Samantha would check in periodically with Alison while Carolyn was away. "Fine and dandy. She's a good decorator, though you wouldn't guess it after a head first slide into second."

"I didn't know you played softball. It sounds like fun. Maybe I'll join up."

"It is." Alison changed the subject abruptly. "Where are you going to go and are you going to buy me dinner first?"

"I don't know and yes. How about tomorrow night?"

"Tomorrow night it is. You're taking me to Fra'gelique's."

"I am?"

"I'm the best agent in the world, remember?"

"Right. Okay, well Fra'gelique's it is."

"You can tell me where you're going. If I wasn't in a profession where vacations are unheard of I think I'd go with you."

"We'd have a blast together," Carolyn said.

"Yes," Alison responded quietly. "Yes, we would."

♥

Alison's hand was still on the receiver when the phone rang again.

"I'll get it, Devon — go ahead and do that fax," Alison said. "McNamara Literary," she said into the receiver, half-expecting, half-hoping it was Carolyn again. Maybe Carolyn would beg Alison to go traveling with her.

"She's l-o-v-e-l-y," Sam said breathily. "Why have you been hiding her?"

"She's not a member of the family," Alison said.

"You're joking. I would have sworn she was —"

"She's not." Alison immediately regretted her terse answer. Oh shit. Now Sam would know that Alison had a torch burning for Carolyn Vincense, alias Carly Vincent, author of paperback romances — heterosexual romances.

"Poor you," Sam said.

"You won't tell anyone, will you?"

"Course not. If you're n-i-c-e to me."

"Depends on what you mean."

Sam's laugh was low and sultry.

♥

"I've been here fifteen minutes, sitting right around the corner," Alison whispered in Carolyn's ear. She put her lips close – an extremely cheap thrill, she had to admit.

Carolyn spun around on her barstool in a swirl of skirt and leg that made Alison's heart skip a beat. "I looked for you," Carolyn defended herself. "I've been here almost ten minutes."

"Well, you didn't look hard enough," Alison said, with a tiny pout. "I hate bars like this."

"So do I, but you picked the place. It was so fancy that I decided I would dress up for a change but you'd think these guys had never seen nylons before."

"Ignore the pond slime." Alison had chosen the restaurant for the quiet booths in the dining room. She was hoping the intimate atmosphere would help Carolyn see that their relationship could be more — intimate.

They sidled their way through the bar toward the sanctuary of the restaurant. Despite their bee line for the door, a lounge lizard with a practiced look of sincerity moved his chair into their path.

"Ladies," he said, "you look like you could use some companionship for dinner."

Alison couldn't keep her lip from curling. She heard Carolyn mumble a negative response but her own answer drowned Carolyn out. "I'm Thelma. This is my friend Louise. We're just fine the way we are."

"But you look lonely, and I'm ready to be your friend," he said, with a charmer's smile.

Alison gave a visible shudder and put her hand on Carolyn's arm, pulling her past him. "Isn't it amazing what they're doing with plastic reptiles these days? It's so lifelike," she said loudly. She left the dusty print of her shoe on his leather loafer.

"You constantly amaze me," Carolyn said when they were securely tucked into their booth. "I never know how to respond to creeps like that. Not that I know why they bother."

"And you constantly amaze me," Alison said. She looked over the candle into Carolyn's warm blue eyes. She imagined that waking up next to that face would be like waking up to sunshine. "You don't realize how much attention you do attract. You're oblivious to it." *Like you're oblivious to me and the way you make my heart and other body parts behave.*

"Every man in there was watching you," Carolyn said.

"I don't care what any man wants," Alison answered. She caught Carolyn's gaze and held it. She opened her mouth to say what she'd been rehearsing for too many years.

"Would you like a cocktail before ordering," an unctuous voice interrupted.

She slowly transferred her gaze from Carolyn to the waiter, adding what Carolyn had always called the Killer Laser Scan. The waiter wilted.

"I'll come back in a few minutes," he said, scurrying away.

"You should get those eyes licensed as a lethal weapon," Carolyn said, color staining her cheeks and forehead — had she sensed some of what Alison was longing to say?

"I wish they were sometimes." She tried to smile despite the frustration of coming-outus interruptus. Just when she had finally found the right moment, and had the right words to say — well, who was she kidding? There had been right moments before. If only Carolyn weren't so very dense. *And if I wasn't so afraid of losing her.* "Sorry. You're the host — I shouldn't have sent him away."

"That's okay. I don't want a drink. But would you pick out something nice to go with dinner? I trust your wine palate implicitly."

"You may regret giving me carte blanche. Oh my, the fresh fish is lobster tails. Just the sort of thing the best agent in the world likes."

"I brought the credit card with the highest limit. Let's pig." Carolyn smiled and wiggled her eyebrows suggestively. Alison found it utterly adorable and endearing — the gush of mushy feelings that coursed through her almost put her off her food.

Alison fluttered her eyelashes and said, "There's this wine I've been dying to try —"

"It's yours." Carolyn closed her menu and snuggled against the cushioned back of the booth. "Want to split a Caesar Salad?"

"Absolutely. They toss it at the table." Alison let her eyes trace the line of the turquoise silk shirt that shimmered every time Carolyn moved. She followed the slender shoulders to the passing swells that made the palms of her hands itch. She wondered if she were no better than the pond slime in the bar, but decided she was because she loved Carolyn and would respect her in the morning, every morning, for the rest of their lives. "I think it's supposed to be romantic."

"And garlic is supposed to be an aphrodisiac." Carolyn laughed. "Remember that someone told us the fraternity guys would serve peeled garlic and green M&Ms at the parties — thank God we never went to one. Where do these mad ideas get started?"

So much for my subtle lead-in, Alison thought. And so the conversation went on. She rarely felt that rush of connection she longed for whenever she was with Carolyn, but it happened just often enough to keep Alison hoping. And it happened infrequently enough to keep her praying for a cure.

The food was ideal, however. The waiter had learned his lesson and approached with great caution. But ideal moments did not arrive. Alison knew their dinner out together was going to end as they all had since Carolyn's marriage — no trip to the store for Sara Lee cheesecake. No Katherine Hepburn movie. No nothing. The cool night air and the ever present hum of the nearby freeway did great damage to the mellow glow she'd developed toward the end of the wine. Just as well.

"So why won't you tell me where you're going?"

"Because it's a secret," Carolyn said. "But I do intend to come home in one piece this time — physically and emotionally."

Alison reluctantly unlocked her car door, but she didn't open it. She turned to look at Carolyn in the dim light of the parking lot. "If you don't, you know I'll help you put yourself back together."

"I know," Carolyn said quietly. "I know."

Suddenly, Alison's fantasies came true. Carolyn reached for her, embraced her. Her breath whispered past Alison's ear while Alison's heart stopped at the press of Carolyn's upper body against hers. The silk shirt transmitted the warmth of Carolyn's breasts to Alison's. She was no fool. She embraced Carolyn in return, pulling tighter. She wondered if she moaned as she drew Carolyn's hips to her own, rocking slightly.

"Oh, Ally," she heard Carolyn sigh. "You're the best friend a girl ever had. I don't know what I'd do without you."

About thirty minutes later Alison looked blearily into the bathroom mirror, and marveled at how natural her laugh and ungay banter had seemed. It hadn't been easy to let go of a body lock no lesbian would have mistaken for anything but the full-fledged Take Me I'm Yours. But Carolyn had been oblivious, as usual.

She brushed her teeth, gums and tongue vigorously, but still woke up with severe garlic breath. It was not romantic.

♥

Carolyn slammed her '65 Mustang into reverse and angled in for a perfect parallel parking job. She gave herself a high five for finding one of the two free parking spaces in all of midtown. She hadn't told Alison where she was going because she didn't know yet. She intended to spend the entire morning at the travel agency if necessary, until she found the right trip to put some momentum back into her life.

The sun was hot on her back as she walked past 22nd Street. Every time she stepped into the shade of a tree, the temperature plummeted to fit March in Sacramento. Carolyn shivered, and remembered, without wanting to, the shiver she had felt when she had hugged Alison last night. Again she had a sudden rush of wanting to beg Alison to come traveling with her. Alison was her best friend, and – but – it didn't seem right to cling to her so much. Thinking about Alison made her feel confused, so she replaced Alison's image in her mind with the particularly stunning camellia that hung over someone's fence. At this time of year in Sacramento it was easy to think "Oh, just another camellia," but Carolyn stopped to inhale the delicate scent and appreciate the unusual silver-pink color. After a few deep breaths she remembered where she was and why she was going there — and couldn't imagine why she had stopped to smell flowers.

Alison had referred Carolyn to Linda's Travel years ago and she had never been disappointed. Linda loaded Carolyn with stacks of brochures and left her to mull over options in peace. With her earnest desire to avoid a repeat holiday-romance situation, Carolyn rejected any brochures that featured hand-in-hand couples strolling down sandy beaches, reveling in sepia sunsets or bluer than blue waves. She was momentarily nonplused at a brochure that featured two women walking hand in hand — well, she thought, it's not my cup of tea, but they look like they're having fun. She studied the picture one last time before she set it aside. She put one brochure on Russia and another on New Zealand in the possibilities pile and reached for the second stack.

On top was a brochure for the *Orchestral Tour of Europe*. She froze. It sounded wonderful, but did she really want to go back to Europe? Well, she could just avoid Paris. When she opened the brochure her fingertips prickled. She'd hear the world-renowned orchestras of Europe — Rome, the Salzburg Mozart Festival, Wagner in Munich. Alison would have hated it.

She decided to trust her instincts. "This sounds wonderful," Carolyn said aloud. Linda immediately reached for the brochure and examined the fine print. "I do know enough French, Italian and Spanish to get by. My German is pretty good."

"You should have been a linguist," Linda said.

"I didn't want to spend my life traveling." Carolyn gaped for a moment, then burst out laughing. "That sounds stupid, doesn't it, when I'm sitting here arranging for a long trip."

"Maybe you just didn't know yourself then," Linda said. "It's never too late to change your life."

"You could be right." The idea of traveling all over the world had scared her to death when she was seventeen and filling out college applications. It didn't seem so bad now. "I don't really want to go back to Paris, but – it wouldn't kill me, I guess. I do want to go everywhere else on the list, like Amsterdam for example."

"I'll start calling hotels. It's late to sign up, but if there's space they might be giving good deals. We just might save a fortune. And I'll see if I can get you out of the bus tour excursions. You know the languages so you won't want to be stuck with a bunch of *tourists*," Linda said. She wrinkled her nose in a teasing fashion as she handed back the brochure. "Here, read the fine print for yourself."

When Carolyn left three hours later she carried a

thick packet of airline and train tickets and reservation slips at hotels Linda said were okay for women traveling alone. When she got home, Carolyn started packing. She was tempted to call Alison but the thought made her slightly breathless. Alison would try to talk her out of it. So she waited until she knew Alison was most likely to be gone and left a message with Devon.

As she went up the jetway into the terminal at Orly International, Carolyn felt as if she were leaving a cloistered life behind. But the butterflies flitting around in her stomach took nose dives every time she thought about the last time she'd been in Paris. She had wanted to put Paris in the middle of the trip so it would seem like just another stop, but the fine orchestras of Europe had their own schedules and would not change them to suit Carolyn. Alison would think she'd taken leave of her senses. When she remembered what she'd done to herself that last trip — maybe she *was* crazy.

Time for remembering later. She had left Paris immediately after the annulment, and this would be her first look at the city without r-o-s-e-colored glasses, as Samantha would say. Time to dredge up the memories later. For now, she was checking into her hotel and getting reacquainted with her French.

She had always been able to pick up portions of the Romance languages easily — as long as everyone stuck to a conversational vocabulary and didn't get too complex with tenses. German was the only language she had a true grip on, after English. Being multilingual made traveling a lot easier, and the itinerary suited her — from Paris she was going to Munich, Amsterdam (though her Dutch was shaky at best) and Madrid, then Salzburg for Mozart, and a final week-long flourish in Rome. The tour arrangers had gladly set aside Carolyn's tickets for the concerts, but had been unable to get her a seat on the various bus trips and tours — oh, what a damned shame, Linda had said — that came with the entire package. She had all the advantages of a tour but no forced relationships and making small talk when she wanted breakfast alone.

"Good afternoon," the desk clerk said in perfect English. He smiled as she responded in her rusty French and handed over her reservation slip and passport. Her French was coming back to her — French was all in the cheeks.

She was surprised when the clerk handed her an envelope with her name. Oh, her concert ticket. "I don't suppose you know what is playing at the Opera House tomorrow night?" She extended her ticket to the clerk for his examination.

He made an inimitable French noise of delight. "I was there last night. Simply incredible, you must go. The guest conductor is superb — a master. He is also staying in the hotel. You will have heard of Nicolas Frost, yes?"

"No, I haven't. I live in Sacramento. That's in California," Carolyn added as if where she lived somehow explained this apparently large gap in her knowledge of the music world.

The clerk favored her with a pitying look. "Even

so you will appreciate it." He rang the bell and waved her key at the bellman. "Enjoy your stay in Paris, *mademoiselle*."

"*Merci beaucoup*." Carolyn smiled at the bellman as they boarded the waiting elevator. As the doors began to close a slender, dark-haired man with a severe frown shoved his arm in and slammed the doors open again.

"*Pardonnez moi*," he muttered in an appalling accent, not looking sorry at all. "*Neuf, s'il vous plaît*."

An ill-mannered American or Brit, Carolyn concluded from the accent. She conversed easily with the bellman, not at all reluctant to show that some foreigners did bother to learn the language and had manners as well. When they reached the ninth floor, Carolyn took a step forward, only to collide with the other traveler.

"After you," the man said with exaggerated patience. Definitely British. He sounded like Ronald Coleman or Alistair Cooke, though not as gracious.

"Oh no, don't let us keep you," Carolyn said. She had no sooner said the words than the man hurried out of the elevator and rapidly strode down the corridor. Some people.

Her room was delightful, however, and she settled in, then dined in the "afternoon" salon — a light but distinctly French meal of cheeses, grapes, consommé and a sweet white table wine. The French wine alone, after an exclusive California wine diet, brought back vivid memories.

She was exhausted and jetlagged, but she wouldn't sleep until she faced the ghosts. She walked to the Arc de Triomphe. She looked around. It seemed that nothing had changed. Boy and Girl had flagged the same cab and after a little arguing, decided to split the ride. Dinner together every night for the next week and dancing until dawn and walking in the parks and meandering through museums with eyes only for each other and so forth — it had seemed the height of romance.

And here, under the Arc, he had proposed, down on one knee, the scent of roses in the air, his fair, golden good looks — the contemplation of which now made her slightly nauseous — radiating in the moonlight. It was the perfect romantic setting, one Carly Vincent wouldn't have written because it was too perfect. But according to Carly's books, the heroine always said yes in perfect romantic settings. So Carolyn had said yes and extended her vacation so they could get married in Paris, the city where they had met. What more could a girl have wanted?

Shivering, she walked back toward her hotel, deep in reflection. On her wedding night she had waited for passion to arrive and sweep her away. After the first week the only thing that had arrived was a bladder infection, followed by a cessation of conjugal activity. After the second week, when it had become apparent he also felt they had made a mistake, she had stopped trying to please him. There was no spark for her and she couldn't pretend. She didn't know why she should have to.

She knew he'd find release anyway — it seemed so much easier for men. The proof of his arousal was always evident, but she had somehow never believed she was the cause. He'd been hurt when she'd tried to talk about how – unessential she felt. It was easy to pretend the marriage had never happened, except she knew it had. She sometimes wondered if he thought about it too, or if he'd gone back to Chicago and gotten married to a woman who could please him. And she was devoutly grateful she had not gotten pregnant.

She hadn't set out to retain her virginity for thirty years, but she had. Squirming out of embraces had been an instinctive reflex because she'd believed that waiting meant her wedding night would be so much more wonderful. Romance had been in books and movies and pop records during her teen years. She had worked happily in her father's construction firm as Woman Friday while she completed her English and languages major, then went on for her master's in English.

She'd met Alison in college and their enduring friendship had blossomed into a strong business relationship as well. It was Alison, after going into business for herself, who had encouraged her to spin out one of her short stories to a full-length romance novel, and then had used her own talents of persuasion to sell it. Exhilaration had been tinged with grief — her father's death, following only a year after her mother's, and the contract for her first book had come within weeks of each other.

Writing, reading and watching movies had been her existence ever since. In all that time she had never felt that elusive spark other women seemed to talk about all the time – the spark her heroines supposedly felt. The same spark Carly Vincent had been able to describe so vividly because Carolyn had thought it existed. But in practice, Carolyn had found Alison's company a lot more interesting than any of the men at the gym Alison dragged her to.

She stopped in an all-night bakery for some eclairs and, on the last block to her hotel, decided again that she must be frigid. It was the only thing that made sense. She didn't exactly know how to go about proving her theory, but she accepted it as fact. Her fantasies had always been hot, but she couldn't even get up much interest in her old tall-dark-and-handsome fantasies anymore. The only rush of emotion she'd felt lately was overwhelming friendship for Alison. But that was completely natural.

Back in her room, tired to the bone, Carolyn stared at her reflection in the mirror. So very ordinary to look at: her eyes were a faded blue, and her hair was dishwater blonde no matter what Alison said. Alison — she could understand why anyone would go for Alison. She really did have that raven black hair and a womanly figure that had driven poets mad for centuries. She didn't have Alison's strength and vitality, nor Samantha's panache and glamour. She chuckled. Nor did she have, to her immense relief, her brother's ears.

She gobbled her eclairs greedily as she pored over the map of the Palace at Versailles. This trip she would be a tourist and nothing else.

3

Fanfare

"But what the hell am I supposed to do about the performance?" Nick roared. Her voice almost broke with the effort, but she had the satisfaction of seeing almost everyone in her line of sight wilt around the edges. She'd worked on that roar.

The Signorina, however, did not wilt. After tucking her violin carefully under one arm, she let loose with a string of words that ran together so quickly Nick could only pick out *"cacasenno"* and the general summing up, *"figlio d'una mignotta."* All in all, Nick gathered from these phrases (and the gestures accompanying them) that since she exuded wisdom, Nick could solve her own problems, and, in case there was any doubt, Nick was a son-of-a-bitch. The Signorina exited, but not before Nick threw a hearty *"quel coglione di tuo padre"* after her, equalizing the parental gender slurs.

After much pacing, and three false starts, the concertmaster filled in the first violin in the Mozart concerto adequately, but just adequately. Signorina Gabrielle, the violinist from hell, was unmatched for the Mozart. Nick endured the rehearsal but knew she would be eating crow from now until the concert to ensure the guest violinist's performance.

Nick slammed back to the hotel, as usual not caring about running into buildings, light poles, benches or people. Anger, she had learned, kept her façade from crumbling. The only alternative she had to anger was a torrent of tears, and there was no place to hide while she had her purge.

So she stayed angry, swearing at pedestrians in a variety of languages. Dealing with temperamental musicians had given her a wealth of foreign language expletives. Nick didn't know what she'd done to deserve the Great Violinist Bitch of All Time, but whatever it was must have been a real peach. She comforted herself with a vision of the future wherein she would call Itzhak Perlman, explain her problem, and Itzhak would promise to be on the next plane.

But it wasn't the future, it was a dismal present at only the beginning of a too-long concert tour. Nicolas Frost was still up-and-coming in a world

that didn't notice you until you had reached the top.
And right now the last thing Nick needed was a
violinist with Mystery Illness Number Two. Maybe
dressing like a man for five years was beginning to
make her think like a man. Somewhere deep down
she knew that if a man had complained she'd have
consented to a light rehearsal without comment —
Gabrielle need only have asked reasonably and Nick
would have been reasonable. Instead, Nick's hackles
had been raised by that weak-little-me routine
Gabrielle had put on. Her suggestion that Gabrielle
try suffering for her art had led to the slanging
match, which had surely amused the other
performers. Nothing breeds discipline like being
called a son-of-a-bitch in front of the entire
orchestra. Nick had wanted to retort that she had
just as many X chromosomes as the next woman,
but it was impossible. Nicola Furst was considered
an intriguing new breed of conductor with flashes of
genius well-suited to the podium.

Remembering how lightly her ambition of
becoming a conductor had been treated when critics
had known she was a woman gave Nick a
permanent source of bad temper and inner steel that
critics and performers now called temperament. As
long as she was unpleasant and imperious, glowering
down on most people from her almost six-foot height,
no one seemed to suspect that underneath the tie
and boxer shorts was the strength and resilience of
pure womanhood. Sometimes she forgot, too — until
she slid into her pajamas. In the night with herself
and her fantasies, she was one hundred percent

woman. With concentration she could make herself forget that two hundred percent woman in her bed would be an excellent way to pass the time.

She threw open her hotel room door and slammed it behind her. Breathing hard, she looked for something to stay angry at. Oscar looked up from the *London Times*.

"You have sent orchids," he said dryly, "with a card saying they are as remarkable as her Mozart. It would be true and I knew you would not vomit."

"How did you know the rehearsal — never mind. You're amazing," Nick said. All of her tension melted out of her as she thanked her good fortune, once again, that Oscar Smythe had decided that Nick would be the next Bernstein if it killed him — and/or Nicola — in the process. It had been more years ago than Nick liked to remember.

"I happened to ask after the Signorina's health in the elevator. I'm glad I don't speak Italian. She was quite vocal."

"Orchids will cost a fortune and she's not worth it." Nick threw herself into a chair.

"But her Mozart is. And think what a feather in your cap if you can handle her temperament."

"I thought my cap already had all the feathers you said I'd need," Nick said testily. "Sometimes I just want to chuck it all in the bin." She waved a slender hand at the pants she wore.

"Of course you would, darling," Oscar said. "But you do hate Light Opera so. You'd have to go back to the violin and when the paparazzi were through with you you'd be performing with a monkey and tin cup as well. And I'd be out of a job," he added. "What would a has-been like me do without a prize protegé like you for financial support?"

"You'd find some other sucker with delusions of grandeur to listen to your crazy schemes," Nick said, but her lips curled upward slightly.

"Well, if you are going to start blaming everything on me again, I shall ignore you and read my paper. The review of last night is satisfactory considering this cretin has a tin ear."

"Anyone who doesn't say it the way you would is a cretin to you."

"I have standards," Oscar said, his tone and expression indicating that he was not joking.

Somehow Oscar's drier than dry wit always cheered Nick up. "You know what I'm going to do?" Nick looked up at Oscar with a grin. "I'm going to find someone in this town to make me a real lemon squash."

Oscar exhaled with bored emphasis. "I'll alert the media," he said in precise tones.

"John Gielgud, right? Very good."

"Quite," Oscar said. "And before you go out, comb your hair down again. It's curling. I shall make an appointment for you with the hotel barber."

Nick did as she was told and gelled her hair back. The severity hardened the angles of her face. The style was the signature of what the press labeled a new breed. Of course the media did not even begin to guess just how new a breed Nick really was.

♥

Alison looked down at the air mail envelope in disbelief. What had possessed Carolyn to go back to Paris? With all the world to choose from, why Paris, for God's sake? Why not just roll around in some broken glass and salt if she wanted to suffer?

Still, it was a letter, and Alison had to smile when she heard Bonnie Raitt's "Love Letter" start up on the radio. The moment of fantasy was exquisite, but a love letter from Carolyn — not likely.

Dear Alison:

The postmark will tell you where I am. So far everything is as I expected and you can just wonder what I mean by that.

You'll be vexed to know I spent my second night in Paris at the Symphony. To hear real, live *music again! It was sublime. The Mozart was magnifique with a marvelous woman violinist and a young conductor — I'm sure he'll be famous one day and I'll get to say I saw him when. Sedate little me jumped to her feet and shouted "Encore!" I know you hate music written before this century, but I do love it. What do I have to do to get you to go with me? I should never have stopped going by myself.*

There were very few activities Alison could imagine more boring than watching identically dressed people sawing on pieces of wood, with, no doubt, interplay so subtle as to render one moment indistinguishable from the next until it was impossible to keep one's eyes open. Of course it meant she could spend an evening with Carolyn – no, it wasn't worth it.

The coincidence here is that the conductor,

Nicolas Frost, shared an elevator ride with me and is he ever a rude boor. Very, very superior and nasty to work with I'll bet. (Isn't the missing "H" a little pretentious? Probably a stage name. I get to sneer because I didn't choose my pen name — you did. Carly indeed. Thank God you never call me that.) But he does get results. The reviews this morning were raving. Supposedly he's a young gun just as Bernstein was thought of in his youth. I almost cried over the Mozart.

Alison remembered when Carolyn had cried over *The Wizard of Oz* the last time they'd watched movies together. She'd finally gone to hug her because Carolyn wouldn't stop crying. Eventually, she'd fallen asleep in Alison's arms. Not trusting herself, Alison had covered her and left. And Carolyn hadn't invited her over or referred to the incident since.

Anyway, he is a very good conductor, and he's really cultivated the tortured artist look, which goes along with the missing H.

Alison glanced at the photo on the program Carolyn had enclosed. To her surprise, she found Nicolas Frost slightly attractive around the edges. Perhaps it was because he had an androgynous look — long, dark eyelashes, punkish slicked back hair, a long nose. His face could probably be extremely expressive — although Carolyn was right, the thin-lipped pose in the photo was Tortured Artist to the hilt. The biographical notes said he had "burst on the musical scene" during a competition sponsored by many important-sounding organizations and had since set a new standard of daring and intensity, blah, blah, blah. Ain't that grand, she thought. Carolyn had the model for her next hero, and *Carly* would fall in love with him while she writes the damn book and she'd have to listen to *Carly* sing his praises until it was finished.

Sometimes Alison hated Carly Vincent. She had thought Carly Vincent would draw Carolyn Vincense and Alison McNamara closer — it gave her the perfect cover for being a continuing part of Carolyn's life, year after year, without Carolyn suspecting how important she was to Alison. Of course if Carolyn would just be a little suspicious, then Alison might have found a little courage. Unrequited love was the pits, and she had tried several cures — Maureen and Betsy came to mind. But just when she thought she was cured, Carolyn would do something to lure her back, like dressing up for dinner with her and hugging her. Alison's body felt the imprint.

To top off the evening I had not one but two eclairs from an all-night bakery — second night in a row, too. Yes, I know white sugar is a slow poison but I don't really care. Not in Paris. At least they weren't Twinkies. Something about Paris goes to my head, and since I know that, you may rest assured that my only indulgences will be eclairs. And Champagne.

I'll say au revoir now so I can drop this in the box. I'm writing in the hotel drawing room that has Louis XIV desks and dainty chairs for letter writing — how continental I feel. I'm not sure why I'm writing at all, except that I wanted to pick up the phone and tell you all about everything. Au revoir —
Carolyn

Alison tucked the letter into the breast pocket of her suit. When she got home she hid it under her socks.

♥

Carolyn woke up in a sweat. The clock on the bedside table read three-fifteen a.m. She was feverish but didn't know what had woken her until a searing pain in her stomach sent her groping for the bathroom. She made it just in time. She tried to pull herself together by brushing her teeth and pretending that throwing up was an accident, and she wasn't going to do it again. She was wrong.

Several hours later she had nothing left in her stomach. No matter how often she rinsed out her mouth the taste of eclair cream came back, which didn't help the nausea. *Aliment empoisonnement,* she thought. Food poisoning. I'd have been better off with Twinkies, she told herself. They never spoil.

Still, she couldn't keep down the clear broth or tea she ordered from room service when they opened in the morning. She woke up a few hours later and managed to ingest the hard bread that had come with the soup. She went to sleep again and woke at noon.

Determined not to waste a day of her vacation, she showered but found she didn't have the energy to dress. Her nightshirt was a mess, so she put on a T-shirt and sweatpants, hung the do-not-disturb sign on the door, and crawled back into bed. Okay, a lazy day dozing wasn't too bad a prospect.

She was almost asleep when the argument

started in the next room. In Italian. She could make out a husky voice with an atrocious accent carrying on about breach of contract. Then a piercing feminine voice let loose with words Carolyn could barely translate — she understood the part about bad parentage and excrement for brains. A third voice, in German, interjected a burning desire to get the whole unintelligible-but-heartfelt-adjective *prüfing* — trial, ordeal — over with as quickly as possible.

She groaned and buried her head under the pillow, but she could still hear them. She debated calling the manager but blissful silence fell. She propped herself back up on her pillow and relaxed.

Then a rhythmic banging began and, then, with a nerve-wrenching skirl of strings, persons unknown launched into a furious onslaught of noise. It was so angry and discordant that Carolyn couldn't even call it music. It sounded exactly like Carolyn's stomach felt. She sat upright in rage. Didn't they have any consideration?

Wobbling on her feet, Carolyn went over to the adjoining door and opened her side. She listened, and suddenly the music stopped. Then it started at the beginning again. Her head was pounding so she pounded her fist on the door to match the rhythm, then caught herself on the frame as a wave of dizziness washed over her.

Nick wrenched open the suite's adjoining door. First, she was paying for that room so as to have a measure of privacy. Second, whoever was in the room had no business banging on the door. She was not prepared for the T-shirted, sweatpanted, barefooted woman who stumbled into the room.

"Good lord," the woman said in English.

An American. Nick favored the invader with the gaze she reserved for uppity violinists. "What is all that bloody racket?"

"Racket? Racket?" The woman glared up at Nick with blue eyes that reminded Nick of robin's eggs. "What the hell do you call what's going on in here?"

"Mozart," Nick said, frowning fiercely. Robin's eggs? Where in the world had such a sappy, sickening comparison come from? She was losing her sanity. She'd never even *seen* robin's eggs.

"Good lord," the woman said again. She looked beyond Nick and seemed to realize she had interrupted something. She at least had the grace to go pale and look apologetic. Her eyes *were* very blue.

Actually, Nick thought, taking into account the T-shirt that was just a little too tight in the right places – NO, *nein*, uh-uh, no way, *nunca, non, nyet, nada*. Stop that right now, she ordered herself. No fantasies, no wondering if you could sneak out into a woman's arms for a night — oh no, you promised.

Gathering her usual ill-humor, Nick went on, "That racket is the overture from Mozart's *Magic Racket*." She did not smile. "We're rehearsing in here."

"Well, I'm throwing up in there," the woman said. "I'd like to do it in peace."

Priceless! She should go on the stage. "What do you know, Gabrielle," Nick said in her halting Italian. "Your Mozart has made someone sick."

"Not *my* Mozart — his," Gabrielle said, gesturing

at the other violinist whom she had insisted needed the extra rehearsal.

"I'm not going to stand for this," Kruger snarled, while Oscar threw his hands up. The two performers shot nasty phrases at each other again. Nick forgot the woman in the doorway as she shouted for silence.

The woman followed her all the way into the room and said a distinctly nasty phrase in German.

Nick stopped short — more aspersions on her parentage. Her parents, looking down on their daughter from parts unknown — or in her father's case, looking up — were probably having fits. Kruger and Gabrielle gaped and were then blessedly silent. Oscar stifled a laugh, but Nick saw nothing funny.

"*Fraulein*," Nick said, with feigned patience. She used every inch of her height to tower over the intruder. The top of the woman's head came precisely to Nick's shoulder. Now the woman looked familiar — oh, the little-miss-show-off-polished-schoolbook-accent creature from the lift. "*Mademoiselle?*"

"*Ms*. Vincense, if you please," the woman snapped. Bloody hell, some American virago. The woman took a deep breath, then paled — guilt at interrupting a rehearsal, no doubt. Her next words proved Nick's theory. "The concert last night was wonderful."

Nick continued to stare at her skeptically. She was beyond idle flattery, and — with more effort than she liked to admit — completely resistant to female charms. "Perhaps then you'll understand why rehearsing is so important. Tonight is the finale. And perhaps you'll explain what you're doing in the hotel room I'm paying for?" Out of the corner of her eye she saw Oscar suddenly start forward, but he stopped. Gabrielle wanted to rehearse, so rehearse they would.

"*Au contraire,* I am paying for that room," the woman said. "And I don't see why you have to practice next to where I'm trying to sleep."

Nick looked pointedly at her watch, then said, by way of the only apology she'd give, "The hotel was not supposed to rent out that room to avoid this problem."

The woman started to reply, but Nick saw her gaze focus on the room service cart with the eclairs she'd ordered for Gabrielle, who had then of course refused them. If Nick hadn't ordered them Gabrielle would have been slighted.

Nick realized right about then that the woman wasn't naturally pale. She went from white to green and then ran from the room, slamming her own adjoining door shut. Shortly thereafter Nick could hear the dim sound of retching.

"Rehearsal is over. Over," she repeated imperiously. She gritted her teeth. "Gabrielle, you really have no reason for concern. Your performance will be as stunning as your reputation." Let her take that any way she likes.

Oscar closed the door, then turned to Nick. "Shall I let the manager know how unhappy we are with their little cock up?"

"Certainly. I don't intend to pay one franc for that room for the entire time we've been here. Thank goodness we're leaving in a few days!"

Nick went into the bathroom and gulped down

some headache tablets. She heard Oscar explaining, in his dry fashion, how critical the rehearsal had been, what the interruption had done to the Maestro's nerves and what the hotel could do to ease the strain. She leaned out of the bathroom and said, "I don't think the woman in the next room should have to pay for it either. She's been just as inconvenienced."

Oscar passed that on and mentioned that the Maestro knew many people who would be shocked to learn that a hotel of this stature had double-rented a room — No, no it was not necessary to send the Maestro a bottle of wine. Correcting their folio, and the folio for Ms. Vincense next door, would be sufficient.

Nick looked at herself in the bathroom mirror. *If the barber had cut it any shorter you'd look like Yul Brynner. And you can just forget all about this unexpected meeting with a woman who probably looks even better when she isn't sick –* Nick silenced the thought with a wave of a mental baton. There was no future in it.

♥

"Another airmail from Paris," Devon said, his voice thick with insinuation.

"Oh, give me that," Alison said. She snatched at the envelope, but he held it away. "Give it to me right now or I'll tell your old man you keep a spare package of condoms in your desk."

"Oh!" Devon said in disgust. "Tacky, very tacky." He handed over the letter. "Besides, when I work

late sometimes he picks me up. Pun intended —
you'd never guess what goes on after you leave for
the night, to your solitary and sterile bed."

"Tacky, Devon. Have you faxed that stuff to New
York yet?"

Devon's look left no doubt as to what Alison
could do with her fax. If she didn't like Devon so
much she'd probably hate him. She retired to her
office and opened the letter. Maybe Carolyn was
realizing how much she missed Alison.

Dear sane and sensible Alison:

*I know I should never have come back to Paris.
When I leave the day after tomorrow it will be two
days too late! Would you believe the second set of
eclairs was bad? I've been sick all night and to make
things worse I was subjected to the most appalling
argument with none other than Nicolas Frost. I was
trying to sleep after puking all night and he had a
rehearsal in his room, which is next to mine. He
made some lame excuse about the hotel making a
mistake, and that no one was supposed to be in my
room. Hah. I gave him a few choice opinions in
German, then I almost lost it on his Italian leather
loafers and it would have served him right.*

*By the time you get this I'll be all better, and
well on my way to Munich. I hope I've recovered
enough to do the Louvre tomorrow, after which you
will receive a letter all about art. No more throwing
up or Nicolas Frost whom I hope I never see again.
You would have been quite proud of me. Green and
lamentable —*

Carolyn

Alison laughed. She adored Carolyn's proficiency
with German expletives, even though she never knew

what the heck they meant. She folded the letter back into the envelope. She missed Carolyn.

"Sam Beckwith is on the line again," Devon called, interrupting the poor-baby thoughts Alison was sending in the general vicinity of Paris. "Maybe I was wrong about the solitary and sterile bed."

"Shut up, Devon," Alison warned in a tone she knew Devon would ignore. "Hi, Sam," she said sweetly. She could hear Devon laughing.

"Ally, I think I may have found a wonderful b-e-d frame for Carolyn."

"Oh, I don't know, Sam. I – does she need a new one?"

"The one she has now is adorned by a Barbie-like ballerina. It's difficult to decorate around."

"Well –"

"Meet me tomorrow to take a look and then we'll catch some d-i-n-n-e-r somewhere. You pick a restaurant." Sam's voice was encouraging and Alison wondered, yet again, if Sam might be the cure she was looking for. They were good friends already.

"Okay. Where should I meet you?"

When Alison hung up, after settling the details with Sam, she could hear Devon whistling "Strangers in the Night." She called out, "Shut up, Devon."

He changed the tune to "She Loves You."

♥

Nicolas Frost was an unpleasant, uncivilized jerk. Carolyn's writer persona had recorded useful physical details. The gray eyes, long eyelashes and smooth skin — well, none of it went with a personality that was about as endearing as boils.

She ordered a cup of broth and bread and ate it with more success than the last batch. Feeling almost human she decided to take a bath. She had just finished setting out her bath paraphernalia and her book when there was a knock on the door. She peeked through the peephole, rewrapped her robe tightly around her and opened the door. It was the older man she had seen in the next room — the only one who had looked at her with anything like sympathy.

"With Maestro Frost's compliments," he said gravely, in his cultured English voice. He sounded like Ralph Richardson. He carried in a huge basket of yellow roses. "He is very sorry about the inconvenience and hopes you are feeling better."

"These really weren't necessary," Carolyn said. Roses were not her favorite flower, not anymore.

"They are just a token. Maestro Frost is very sorry you were subjected to that brawl. He has arranged for the hotel not to bill you for this room since they should not have put you in it in the first place."

Carolyn was astounded. "It wasn't necessary, but thank you."

"I would like to inquire," he went on as if Carolyn had not spoken, "if there is anything I could arrange that would speed your recovery? You do appear a little less pale." He smiled faintly.

"I think I ate some bad eclairs. I've had some broth. It's not Mom's chicken soup, but I'm recovering."

"Very well, I will leave you to rest."

"Thank you for bringing the roses, Mr. — I don't know your name, I'm sorry," Carolyn said.

"I am Oscar Smythe," he said. He said his name as if it should be familiar to her — it tugged at Carolyn's memory.

"Did you conduct a complete recording of Brahms with the Vienna Philharmonic? A long, long time ago?"

"I'm not sure I would have repeated the adjective, but yes, I did do that recording some years ago."

"It's still my favorite. I've been listening to it since my mom bought it for me when I was a little –"

"Please," he said, holding up one hand with great dignity. "Thank you. For an American I must say you show remarkable judgment." His voice was devoid of irony, but Carolyn saw a flash of it in his eyes. He bowed like David Niven, tipped an imaginary hat and left.

Carolyn closed the door. "What a character," she said to the roses.

She had a long soak in the tub, turning the pages of *The Mists of Avalon* as she swished her toes in the hot water. When she went back into the bedroom it reeked of roses. She sneezed twice, then dialed for a bellman.

The sooner she got out of Paris, the better. Her train to Munich was scheduled for the day after tomorrow. She couldn't wait to put some distance between herself and the problems Paris seemed to cause her.

The young man who came for the roses was overwhelmed and thanked her profusely. "Good riddance," Carolyn muttered as she closed the door.

The next morning, Carolyn ate a bland breakfast and took a cab to the Louvre. She lingered as long as possible over the Da Vincis, only to stop in a daze before the raw magnificence of Van Gogh's *Flowers in a Copper Vase*. Around every corner was art she'd only seen photographs of – all the painting and sculpture she would have seen on her last trip if only romance hadn't gotten in the way. She edged forward toward the Van Gogh, vaguely aware that she was nudging another woman.

The blonde woman gave ground with a sarcastic *"Pardonnez moi."*

Carolyn blinked, clearing her eyes of the violent, overwhelming hues. "My fault," she replied in French. "I was so struck by the work –"

The woman's blue eyes softened and she gave Carolyn a toothy smile. "I understand." Her smile broadened as she glanced past Carolyn. "There you are, Cherié, where have you been?" Another woman, as dark-skinned as the first was fair, stepped around Carolyn and the two women exchanged kisses on each cheek in French fashion, and then they stepped away from the painting.

Carolyn took advantage of the extra room and leaned closer to examine the painting. She made a mental note to make time in Amsterdam for the Van Gogh Museum.

"Cherié, not here," Carolyn heard the blue-eyed

woman say. Some note in the woman's voice made Carolyn turn. The black woman was toying with the collar of the blue-eyed woman's shirt, her long fingers slipping inside the collar and brushing tenderly against the pale skin. The hair at the nape of Carolyn's neck prickled and she shivered.

"Let's go back to the hotel, then," Cherié said. Her voice was low, personal, husky — suggestive of promised delights. Carolyn found she couldn't swallow. The blue-eyed woman swayed as she nodded.

Carolyn realized she was eavesdropping. She was uncomfortably warm – her clothes felt tight. It was the strangeness – she'd never seen two women – it was just different. She made herself move, forcing her attention to another Van Gogh. She studied it as if her personal safety depended on knowing every brush stroke.

By the time she reached her hotel that evening she had mostly forgotten the two women in the Louvre. Her feet ached and she wanted nothing more than to go to sleep, but she still had to pack and get ready for her early train departure the next morning. So she ordered room service again — just crepes without any sauce and a dish of vanilla ice cream. She hoped her stomach could handle that meal.

The waiter was gone before she saw a large bowl of soup on the tray. She double-checked the bill she had signed, but the soup was not on it. Then she saw the florist's card discreetly tucked under the saucer.

I doubt anyone named "Mom" made this, but perhaps it is what the doctor ordered —— N. Frost.

55

"Well!" Carolyn exclaimed. She sniffed. Chicken soup. Her stomach growled. She devoured the soup, then wrote out a tactful and brief thank you note to Oscar Smythe because she was sure that Nicolas Frost hadn't arranged for the soup. He was probably still bullying violinists.

♥

Nick sighed and looked at her itinerary. Paris was only the second stop of her guest conducting tour and she was already tired. To make things worse, she had had a dream last night about a woman with blue eyes who swore at her in German while Nick made passionate love to her. Boxer shorts were comfortable but lately they'd seemed irksome. Did she really want to spend the rest of her life dressed as a man? Didn't she have any other options?

"What is bothering you?" Oscar asked from behind her.

"You're a mind reader," Nick said. Oscar always knew. "What always bothers me when I'm tired."

"Ah. So, sneak out the back way. This is Paris — lesbian bars abound, darling."

"It's too risky. I might be seen out of these damnable boxer shorts."

"Then go in drag," Oscar said. "I'm told it's all the rage."

"And who told you that? Some little number at the local *La Cage aux Folles*?"

"I do not interest myself in little numbers," Oscar

said, at his haughtiest. "And I have not sampled the local – *cages* – in many years. I'm getting too old for it."

Nick smiled fondly. Oscar's favorite role was the aging and forgotten conductor. "You know perfectly well that your gray temples still turn heads."

"Yes, but that child who was here yesterday —"

"What child?"

"Carolyn Vincense — the American girl next door. You sent roses and chicken soup, by the way." At Nick's snort, Oscar continued, "She did remember who I was. She's been listening to my Brahms since she was a little girl."

"So have I, for that matter," Nick said. She bit her lower lip to keep it steady.

Oscar sighed. "Go ahead, laugh. I just hope that when you're my age people will know you for what you're working on at the time, not something you did thirty years ago. And when you're my age maybe being gay won't stand in your way."

"Maybe not, but being a woman probably still will. If they find out I'm a woman *and* gay it'll be double the fun for the paparazzi. I can't go within a hundred meters of a lesbian bar."

"There's always a sex change operation," Oscar said. He went back to studying his correspondence.

Nick said nothing. It was both his age and his sex that kept Oscar from understanding that turning into men was not the way to combat discrimination against women. But who was she to talk — that was exactly what she had done. She might tell herself she was just a part of a long tradition of cross-dressing women in the arts, but her choices weren't anywhere near that clear-cut. And she wasn't just cross-dressing, she was passing as a man.

There were, according to Oscar, quite a few members of the Royal Academy who were gay, but most were completely closeted. Of the women members — and women were far in the minority — Oscar suspected one was a lesbian. A few of the gay men were so gifted or powerful that it ceased to matter. If you were Bernstein, for example, no one picked someone else over you for a recording contract. She knew the label "probably a pouf" had kept Oscar at the very edge of fame. When he had stayed in the role of the critic he had been left alone. But every time he had reached for the baton the whispers had started up again and the offers faded away.

In revenge, Oscar Smythe had become a respected and somewhat feared critic. Nicola Furst had listened and believed when he told her she had talent and then, in the same breath, told her it was a pity no one would ever know — because she was a woman and an intimidating figure of a woman at that. She'd informed Mr. Know-it-All Smythe that he was wrong, but within a few short years she had learned he was right. As a solo violinist she gained only nodding glances and utterly forgettable reviews that never failed to mention her height. No one had expressed anything except boredom when she had conducted. Her attempts at orchestration were "weak" or "shrill." In the meantime, less-talented men she had been at Trinity College of Music with secured First Chair positions, assistant directorships and even Royal Academy memberships.

Nick glanced over at Oscar's disciplined profile. No one would believe her if she told them that the staid and proper English gentleman had been the one to suggest the masquerade. He'd only agreed to hear her because he'd had an affair with one of her mother's uncles (she hadn't known that at the time). She would never have dreamed the interview would result in his urging her to don male attire. Her parents had been killed in a plane crash when she was an infant and the elderly aunt and uncle who raised her had since passed away. The trust fund administrators had ceased all interest in Nicola when she had taken control of her money at the age of twenty-five. Who remembered her from boarding school? Some of her chums might, but only as the gawky girl who never wore skirts and spent every spare hour in a study room with her violin.

Sister Patrick Rose might realize that a photo of Nicolas Frost was also a photo of Nicola Furst, but it was unlikely that a missionary would be attending a European symphony. Yes, indeed, Nick was sure Patrick Rose would remember Nick as vividly as Nick remembered her and her lesson about why a seventeen-year-old Nick was suddenly interested in becoming a nun. Their affair — Nick's first — had been short, tempestuous and delicious, then terminated by Patrick Rose's decision to go to Central America. Nick actually couldn't remember what she had felt like in those days, thinking a nun's life would suit her. She didn't remember being seventeen.

Who would remember her from Trinity? If anyone did, it would be as the woman with a chip on her shoulder. Who cared if Nicola Furst disappeared off the face of the earth? No one. If her trust fund hadn't covered her fees, Trinity would have shown her the door after her second year.

She'd resisted the whole idea. She didn't care that her mannerisms and appearance had always been masculine. She'd told Oscar she loved women and she loved being a woman. And he'd told her how his own variation from the norm had kept his performing career from ever flowering. He'd named more than two dozen gay men in "serious music," as Oscar called it, whose talents were all on the same plane. The ones who were in the closet were a lot richer and more famous than the ones who were suspected or out. Bernstein didn't count.

With Oscar's sponsorship, she'd entered the competition, and when Oscar Smythe sponsored a talented young *man,* the musical world had listened. Nick won the competition, receiving glowing praise from people who hadn't given Nicola Furst a second thought, and became Oscar's protégé. The press ate up the "orphaned son of an old British family" story Oscar fed them, in which Oscar implied he'd raised Nick from childhood, and paid for his schooling and conservatory training abroad. Nicolas Frost's height was never mentioned, but the short, slicked-back hair had attracted a number of comments. Nicolas Frost was courted for his talent, praised for musical sensitivity, and shunned for his reputation as a temperamental maverick. The Royal Academy had indicated interest in Nick, though they had ignored all of Nicola's attempts to get their attention. Now she couldn't afford to answer all the questions on the standard biography form. Besides, at this stage in her life she didn't feel like giving the Royal Academy of Music or its affiliates the time of day.

But critical praise and a flood of eager students had made Nick hungry for more, and more is what she got. Always wearing boxer shorts had seemed a small price to pay, and Oscar was a genius at feeding the press. They staged opportunities for Nick to be photographed with women, and cultivated a reputation for Nick as a heartbreaker. Oscar's greatest fear was not that Nick would be discovered as a woman, but that anyone would think Nick's association with Oscar meant Nick was gay. They had both been hysterical with laughter when a London tabloid had printed a story about a woman who claimed Nick was the father of her baby. Fortunately, it had been her fourth claim in less than a year and no one had even bothered to ask Nick about it. At thirty-three, Nick was famous in London; fifteen years of study and twelve more of hard work had made it so. This tour was supposed to cement her fame in Europe, lead to an American tour and bring Nick to the attention of recording companies.

Nick understood Oscar's fear of Nick's being labeled gay. If she weren't wearing male clothing they'd probably be pretending to be lovers à la Svengali to keep anyone from guessing that Nick was a lesbian. She knew the disguise hid the real drawback — her gender. She could count on one hand the prominent women conductors. She respected them from the bottom of her heart, but she dreamed of going further than any of them would ever be permitted to. Her most sustaining fantasy was of the day she arrived at the pinnacle of success and revealed her womanhood.

"Being a man has limited benefits," she said aloud.

Oscar looked up. "Quite." He studied her for a moment, then with a slight smile, asked if she'd like some tea.

Well, the crisis is passed once more, Nick told herself. She had these soul searchings every so often — but it did seem they were happening more frequently on this blasted tour. Enough, enough, she told herself. It's just being away from the sanctuary of home. It doesn't matter that you're lonely as hell and you have to mail-order clothes and wear suit jackets in raging heat.

As she turned resolutely to the study of Rachmaninoff's *Piano Concerto Number Two*, the centerpiece of the Munich concerts, she flashed on a snippet from the movie *Victor, Victoria*, when the cross-dressing Julie Andrews had complained her bosom would end up looking like two empty wallets. Nick's bosom was well on its way to walletdom.

4

Full Moon and Empty Arms, Opus 18

Carolyn was glad to be away from Paris and truly on vacation at last. The casual beauty of Paris seemed deadly. She stepped from the train into cooler air under a dark Munich sky. She felt a surge of purpose flow through her — an urge to be productive and fertile. Maybe she would make use of the notebook in her suitcase and get some work done on her next book.

The taxi turned a corner onto a view of a modern sculpture garden composed of brightly painted forms. Children swarmed over the smaller creations, sliding across the smooth surfaces. The effect was so unexpected that Carolyn almost laughed. To heck with work – she would find a way to play in sober, austere Munich. Already she'd regained her guttural German accent. French was squeezed out of your cheeks and nose for best effect; German came from the throat.

Her ease with the language earned her a look of respect from the hotel clerk when she saw Carolyn's American passport. The lobby wasn't busy and Carolyn spent almost fifteen minutes chatting with the clerk, who looked like a statuesque heroine from a Wagner opera. By the end of their talk Carolyn knew where the locals ate dinner, where the best shops were and what time the museums were less crowded.

She settled into her room and then took the clerk's advice and went to a small restaurant just outside of the Hofgarten for dinner. The wurst was freshly made with a light mix of spices and accompanied by hard bread smeared with Edam cheese. As in France, fresh fruit was the valued dessert. The ale, served in a heavy stein, was strong and clear. Thoughts of romance and sex and any of that nonsense were miles away.

She plotted her time in Munich carefully and spent the next morning immersed in the Kandinsky and Klee exhibit at the Stadtische Galerie. She sampled the more classic displays of Rubens and

Brueghel the Elder at the Alte Pinokothek and ended the afternoon at the Deutsches Museum, situated on Isar Island, which turned out to be a high tech version of San Francisco's Exploratorium. She'd earned her nephews' undying love by taking them to the Exploratorium for a day of playing with science, and she was sure she'd cement their affections with the well-chosen souvenirs from the Deutsches Museum gift shop.

The next day she took a tour out to the Schloss Nymphenburg. She had no difficulty imagining herself as a Bavarian Princess, at home in lavish rococo rooms filled with living versions of the portraits displayed throughout the Schloss — beautiful women in glorious silk ball gowns. She knew the clothes were much nicer to look at than to wear, but in her imagination the clothes didn't weigh forty pounds and whalebone wasn't squeezing the breath out of her.

She put her hands around her waist and grimaced. There was a soft laugh behind her. She turned and smiled at the small, elderly woman clad in sensible shoes and a functional hat.

"It wouldn't become you," the woman said. "It didn't particularly become her," she added, gesturing at the painting.

"Oh, I know it must have hurt like anything," Carolyn said. "I was just imagining all that squeezing." She felt like a schoolgirl caught doing something silly. She would bet anyone just about anything that the British woman had been a schoolteacher.

"All that pain just for fashion." She made a peculiar, but very British noise of disgust.

"And who are you to talk?" Another woman joined them, clad identically to the first woman, except she wore thick trousers instead of a Harris tweed skirt and support hose. "I've been trying to get Hilary to give up hose and skirts for thirty years, but she won't."

"I'm quite comfortable, June. There's no need to go on about it," Hilary said. Oh, yes, Carolyn thought, definitely a schoolteacher. The tone of voice would have silenced a room of ten-year-olds.

Carolyn spent the rest of the tour with the two older women, enjoying their mini-lectures on history and fashion as much as they appeared to enjoy giving them. Just as she had at every other place, she bought a postcard for Alison. With any luck, Alison would get one a day, sort of like a phone call.

When they got back to the autobus to return to Munich, Carolyn was alarmed to see Hilary pale as she sank into her seat. She began to offer help, but June was already proffering a small cup and canteen of water mysteriously produced from the voluminous satchel she carried. "There you are, dearest," June said. "Why didn't you tell me you were having one of your spells."

"Can I get anything?" Carolyn rose, prepared to ask the driver not to close the doors yet.

"No, no, my dear, she'll be fine once we're back in our room." June put away the water and then patted one of Hilary's hands. Carolyn looked back at them several times as they made their way to Munich, but June never looked up. Her gaze was constantly on Hilary's face. When the autobus stopped, June said softly, "We're here, dearest."

Dearest again, Carolyn thought. She remembered

the women in the Louvre. These two weren't that way — they were older. Yes, they were probably pooling their limited resources for a modest vacation. That was perfectly understandable. Carolyn found herself noticing every movement of June's body as she helped Hilary to her feet. Hilary insisted on walking unaided, but she leaned on June as they made their way down the autobus steps. Carolyn hailed them a cab and waved goodbye. She could see Hilary's head cradled on June's shoulder.

It doesn't mean anything, Carolyn told herself. They were longtime friends, that was all. Not like the women in the Louvre who had definitely been – together. What did it matter to her, anyway? If she didn't hurry, she wouldn't have time for dinner before the concert.

She had enough time, in the end, to walk through the Residenz to the National-theater. Life, she decided, could not be more satisfying. The performance included both Bach and Rachmaninoff, but she wanted to be surprised by the selections. So she ignored her program notes and watched the audience instead. The stately dowager in front of her caught her attention, and Carolyn wished she had a notepad with her to jot down a description of the coiled gray hair adorned with a simple tiara that would have been ludicrous on a younger woman, but was dignified on the older woman. Some writer you are, she thought. She chided herself and closed her eyes to appreciate the tuning strains that began to fill the hall. She liked the mix of sound – there, that snippet from a violin was definitely Rachmaninoff — *Piano Concerto Number 2*. It was buried under a trumpeter's practice scale. Then the musicians quieted and the audience applauded at the entrance of the conductor. She opened her eyes. And blinked.

Nicolas Frost. The tall, slender figure turned, bowed in acknowledgment of the applause, and then gave the upbeat for the first selection. It was a coincidence, but if he saw her, he'd never believe it. He was just egotistical enough to believe that Carolyn was following him around — that she'd eaten rancid eclairs just to get an introduction. She wished she *had* tossed her cookies on his shoes.

She intended not to enjoy herself, but the music couldn't be resisted. At the most, the orchestra had had four days rehearsal with Maestro Frost, but they sounded as if it had been weeks. For an arrogant ass, that man had talent, which seemed unfair somehow. The opening Bach suite was precise without being mechanical. Sort of – like a chocolate truffle — a self-contained, diminutive treat. She sighed as the very last note faded. After a pause while a piano was added to the front of the orchestra, Nicolas Frost swept the performers into the Rachmaninoff. She'd heard it many times, and yet she could almost believe she was hearing it for the first time. When it reached the third movement, featuring the theme someone — not Rachmaninoff — had titled *Full Moon and Empty Arms,* the music was unnervingly passionate without degenerating into sentimentality. Carolyn felt her toes curling in her shoes with the intensity of the longing, lonely tones. Keats had said this kind of music was yearning, like a God in pain.

The concluding Wagner, which followed the intermission, was an unusual mixture of the overture from *Parsifal* and *Seigfried's Funeral March,* arranged and scored by none other than Maestro Frost. Carolyn stayed long enough to applaud through the fourth curtain call, forgetting for the pleasure of the performance that Nicolas Frost was pond slime — as Alison would say.

As she walked back to the hotel she decided it wasn't fair for a jerk like that to have the gift of making such incredibly passionate music. Nicolas Frost hadn't struck Carolyn as the passionate type — angry, but not necessarily passionate. She found herself humming *Full Moon and Empty Arms* and tried, unsuccessfully, to think about something or someone else. But Nicolas Frost's gray eyes haunted her.

♥

Dear A-Woman:

By now you should be deluged with postcards that demonstrate just how touristy I'm being. I was going to tell you all about the München Zoo, but everything has gone completely out of my head because I saw Dachau this afternoon. I can't begin to describe the way I could actually feel death in the air. If I try to describe it I'll start crying again so I'll just tell you what happened while I was there.

I know I promised not to mention Nicolas Frost, but to tell you what happened I have to at least say that his manager, for lack of a better word, is Oscar Smythe, the famous conductor and critic. He sent me chicken soup while I was ill in Paris and he reminds me of Daddy because his eyes twinkle. I know that's corny, but they do.

Alison closed her eyes for a moment. Carolyn's father had been a very nice man, soft-spoken for someone in the construction business, who had cared gently for his ailing wife. A perceptive man, too. Alison had always had the nervous feeling that he knew just how deep her feelings for Carolyn were.

I'm sure Mr. Smythe would vehemently deny any eye-twinkling on his part. Anyway, the whole reason I picked Europe was because of this deal where concert tickets are included for every stop. The concert last night was very romantic — and you won't believe who was conducting. I won't mention the name. I had decided the fates were out to curse me with that arrogant s.o.b., but now I think they wanted me to meet Oscar. He was at Dachau to remember a loved one who died there. It's hard to share the experience of seeing a place like that without feeling closer to the people you're with. We all huddled in one cluster, afraid to be alone, I think. He gave me a handkerchief after I used the last of my tissues. We talked for a long time over an early supper when we got back to Munich, about art, life. He's known so many interesting people — Maria Callas for one, and he was tutored by Solti for a summer. Tomorrow's the last day here for both of us so he's going to go sightseeing with me. He said I have remarkable taste for an American and as long as I don't squeal or take pictures of him in front of landmarks, he'll be glad to escort me. It's going to be fun — I wish we had longer.

You'll be happy to know that I am taking notes on people and places the way you think all "author people" should. Maybe I will get Numero Six-o started when I get back. But then again maybe I

*won't. Sometimes I think I should get a real job and
not live so much in my ivory tower. I hope
McNamara Literary can stand the strain.
Philosophically yours,*

C-Woman

What was she supposed to think? That Carolyn
was finally recovering from the crushing blow that
her brief marriage had dealt her belief system? That
maybe Carolyn was finally growing up — a real late
bloomer? That maybe Carolyn would figure out she
had a different kind of story to live and write?
McNamara Literary would survive.

It astonished her that women could have intense
emotional relationships with other women and never
suspect they might be lesbians. Carolyn had turned
to her when her father died, and again after that
last trip to Paris, but she knew Carolyn had never
considered the possibility of joining their lives
permanently — or their bodies as frequently as
possible. Someday Carolyn would know that urge,
that desire, and then she would feel the searing
delight of truth.

"Sorry I'm late," someone said. Alison jumped,
then said hello to Sam as she put the letter in her
pocket. "Hope you haven't been waiting long."

"Not long. The owner hasn't called the cops for
loitering." Alison scrambled out of her car as Sam
led the way to the "Junque Shoppe." In an ivory
linen suit and brilliant rose blouse, Sam was the
last word in elegance as she stepped around various
chests, bookcases, and tables on her way toward the
rear of the store. "Now be honest. Do you think it's
her?"

They stopped in front of a brass headboard. The

posts curved upward and joined in an arch that curved downward in the middle, like the top of a heart. In the middle brass strands formed a traditional love knot. The four strands of the knot attached to the top and bottom for stability as well as beauty.

Alison swallowed, her imagination going a mile a minute. "Yes, it's her. Classic and romantic, but not red plush velvet, if you know what I mean."

"Umm-hmm," Sam answered as she weighed the price tag in her hand.

"Is that all they're asking for it?"

"It's badly scraped on the back. Someone had a very active sex life." Sam winked.

"Maybe it'll rub off on Carolyn," Alison muttered. Sam glanced at her with something like laughter and pity, and Alison felt herself blushing. "Buy it."

They went to the counter and Sam haggled over the price with the owner. After a few minutes both were happy and Sam wrote out a check. "Come on," Sam said to Alison, "I need those muscles."

"How are we getting this to Carolyn's?" It was heavier than it looked and Alison didn't want to huff and puff in front of Sam. "Won't fit in my car."

"Did you think I drove a v-a-n just to carry softball gear?" Sam didn't appear to be having any trouble with her end. If Alison were to wrestle Sam she'd lose — a prospect that made her lighthearted.

"I'll follow you," Sam said, after they'd cushioned the headboard in some old sheets and blankets in the back of the van.

"If you can keep up," Alison said. She gave Sam an I-dare-you look and hopped into her car. Sam was right behind her when she finally made it to the freeway.

Sam didn't know the shortcuts to Carolyn's and Alison lost her easily. She was grinning in triumph as she rounded the last corner, only to stare dumbfounded at Sam, who was already unlocking the back of the van.

"I've been waiting and waiting," Sam said, her dark eyes glowing with laughter.

"Can't resist a challenge, can you?"

"N-o." Sam's smile was provocative and Alison smiled in return.

They carried the headboard in and rested it against Carolyn's dresser. It had been ages since Alison had been in Carolyn's bedroom. Yes, there was the old ballet-dancer headboard. The room was filled with echoes of Carolyn, right down to the sweatpants folded over a chair, and her worn pink terrycloth bathrobe across the foot of the bed.

"Stop swooning," Sam said. "I think it'll be great, don't you?"

"Perfect," Alison agreed.

"Do you think she'd be upset if I bought her a new mattress?" Sam bent over Carolyn's bed and pressed down. It squeaked. "It has frightful lumps."

"How would you know?"

"Do you doubt me?" Sam turned back, one hand on her hip.

Alison opened her mouth, closed it, then laughed. "Sam, I think I know where we're headed, but I can't think straight in Carolyn's bedroom."

"I don't want you to think *straight*," Sam said.

Alison took a step closer. The lightheaded feeling

she'd had at the antique store came back and translated itself to warmth spreading all over her body. "I just couldn't — not on her bed."

"But we've just got her a new headboard and I'll be getting her a new mattress so it's not going to be her bed any more. It'll be a last hurrah."

"You're screwing with my mind," Alison said, trying to keep her tone light. Her sense of propriety was wrestling with lust. Lust was winning. "You know how I feel about her and if I lie in her bed I'll be thinking about her while you —"

"While I do what I've been wanting to do for a long, long time." Sam's voice dropped into her chest, husky. "I know you'll be thinking about her, maybe at first. I'll take my chances with later."

"Sam —"

Sam kissed her hard. "Any more objections?"

"Are we getting her new sheets, too?" She swayed when Sam let go of her.

"You have a point. I'm tacky, but not that tacky." Sam reached under the corner of the mattress and started pulling. "They'll have to be changed anyway when the new mattresses get here." She stripped the mattress bare and turned back to Alison, pulling Alison slowly toward her. "Let's pretend we're starving in a garret with nothing but our love and a lumpy old mattress to sustain us."

"Sort of romantic-like." Without consciously doing so, Alison found herself sitting next to Sam on the mattress, then they were falling backward. "Oh my God," Alison said. Sam's mouth captured whatever else Alison had been going to say.

It couldn't have been important, Alison thought. She wasn't sure this was even happening. The bed was definitely on the lumpy side, but it was Carolyn's. The bedroom was Carolyn's, but the heavy black hair falling around her was not Carolyn's. The mouth, soft and sweet, could be Carolyn's. Yes, it could be.

Sam's hands went to Alison's breasts and she gave a slight moan. Busy fingers were at the buttons of her blouse, then they brushed her bare stomach. Frantic, she rolled Sam over and tried to pin her down, but as she had suspected, she was no match for Sam's strength. She was on her back again in no time, but Sam didn't resist when Alison reached up and unbuttoned, unzipped, unhooked and pulled away every scrap of clothing she could get her hands on.

They were both breathing hard and loud when at last they were naked and wrapping their arms and legs around each other. Sam moaned as she arched herself against Alison's thigh, then murmured, "I wanted it to be slow."

"No, not slow," Alison said hoarsely. "Fast." She guided Sam's hand to her and then closed her eyes against the images of Carolyn. Her mind played tricks anyway. They were Carolyn's fingers, it was Carolyn's mouth at her breasts, then Carolyn's tongue teasing the insides of her thighs, encouraging her wetness. The moans of excitement, the murmurs of "yes, yes" could have been Carolyn's as Alison gasped and climaxed.

Then she was up off her back, over Sam's tall, lean body. Bending, she buried her face in the curls of black hair spilling over the mattress. She moved to Sam's breasts — dusky rose tips swelled up from the satiny brown of Sam's breasts. She kissed and nipped in increasing frenzy. "Too fast?" Sam clenched her teeth and shook her head and Alison moved down Sam's body to the tight curls and bristles that rubbed against Alison's cheeks, her lips, her nose.

She held onto Sam's hips, her mouth and tongue never stopping until Sam lay still, her breathing ragged. Then Sam drew Alison up into her arms and Alison rested her head on Sam's heaving chest, aware that the moisture on her face was a mix of Sam and her own tears.

Sam rocked her for a few minutes. Her quiet, "Thank you," only made Alison cry harder.

♥

Nick looked up and smiled gently when Oscar came in; she knew where he had gone. The lost Jacob still occupied a special place in Oscar's heart. "You look better than I thought you would."

"I ran into Miss Vincense, the American who almost threw up on you." Oscar went into his room to hang up his coat.

"What is she doing in Munich?" Nick asked when Oscar returned.

"Holiday. She has excellent taste in both music and art so I've agreed to escort her to the various sights tomorrow before she leaves. Despite the fact that you are a boor — her phrase, not mine — she's forgiven me my association with you. It will be delightful to have an attentive student again since you've stopped listening to me." Oscar began to make phone calls to ensure that the obligatory flowers for various performers were on their way to the theater.

Although Nick pretended to study her score, she fumed when Oscar added an order of wildflowers to be delivered to Ms. Vincense at a hotel just down the street.

What was with this Vincense creature? She hadn't struck Nick as particularly interesting — she was probably trying to find any route into the "magic circle." It had certainly happened before. When women got nowhere with Nick they often tried Oscar, who was at least courteous in return, which is more than most of them would say about Nick. Well, Carolyn Vincense wouldn't get very far with Oscar. And if she started showing up in the dressing room – the publicity would be useful as always. Yes, a little publicity was an excellent reason to invite Ms. Vincense to dinner.

♥

Carolyn sorted through the clothes the hotel laundry had returned while she was out. She was one pair of panties short. She stood with her hand on the phone for a while, wondering if she should complain or just go back to writing the latest letter to Alison.

They'll ask me what they look like, Carolyn told herself. And I'll have to confess that they're French-cut fluorescent purple. Of course French-cut might not mean the same thing in Germany. She thought over just how she might explain all of that, in German, without blushing and decided she could buy more underwear. Maybe she could find some with days of the week on them and then she could just say she was missing Saturday or Wednesday, whichever was the case. Of course she hadn't seen Days-of-the-Week underwear since junior high.

She answered the knock at her door and a bellman handed her another laundry parcel and an arrangement of wildflowers, then clicked his heels and departed. Carolyn looked in the laundry parcel — her fluorescent purple French-cut panties were there, along with a shirt she hadn't yet missed. But she thought the flowers were really going overboard as an apology for *almost* misplacing her underwear. Then she saw the card.

Oscar was a very sweet man, though he would probably hate her thinking so. She dialed the number he'd written on the back of his calling card. But it wasn't Oscar's regally accented voice that answered — it was that elusive, modulated voice edged with impatience. She recovered from a momentary loss of speech and asked for Oscar.

"Oscar has gone on some last-minute errands before we leave for the concert. This wouldn't be Ms. Vincense by any chance, would it?"

"Yes, it's Carolyn Vincense. This must be Maestro Frost, how are you?" She decided for Oscar's sake she would at least be cordial. She didn't have to be friendly.

"Fine. I was sorry I didn't get a chance to say goodbye in Paris, but fate has given me another chance, it seems."

"Unless you're going to Amsterdam from here," she said, "in which case I'll see you there."

"No, we're bound for Brussels."

"Well, I don't mean to take your precious time –"

"Not at all," Nicolas's surprisingly charming voice

assured her. Carolyn remembered it when it had not been at all charming.

"Well, if you would thank Mr. Smythe for the flowers and tell him he really shouldn't have —"

"I'm sure it was his pleasure. And it would be my pleasure to take you to dinner tonight, after the performance. It's short notice, but if you have no other plans, I'd be delighted to get you a seat in the conductor's box." Now the voice was warm, cordial. Perhaps he was sorry he'd been so rude in Paris. Besides, she'd get to talk to Oscar over dinner. She could be pleasant to Nicolas Frost.

"I attended last night, but I'd love to sit in your box," she said. Cripes, she sounded like some stage-struck nymphet. She had meant to be merely gracious.

"And dinner afterward?"

"Yes, I'd like that," she replied more sedately. His attitude had certainly changed! Nicolas Frost was — odd.

The view from the box was stunning. Carolyn could see the musicians' every move and the reflection of the pianist's hands in the dark finish of the piano as the fingers rippled out the exquisite Rachmaninoff melody. She could see Nicolas's every gesture, in profile, feel his energy and dynamic presence. His height gave him an extensive reach, arms sweeping out over the orchestra. Otherwise slender and fine-boned, he had broad shoulders.

It was not the body that intrigued her, though, but the hands. Even with Nicolas's hands in gloves

Carolyn could follow the ripple and expression of every finger in the free right hand, as it traced graceful patterns in the air. His left hand alternately gripped and gently held the baton that marked the tempo in a twirling triangle that ended with an unmistakable downbeat. The more she watched the more convinced she was that the real power was in the most subtle movements of the left hand. When Nick's hand clenched the baton the basses surged. If the baton held for even a heartbeat at the top of the triangle pattern the musicians would lean forward slightly, then slump back to their instruments with renewed passion and artistry when the baton fell.

Enthralled, Carolyn watched as Nicolas seemed to pour every emotion into the musicians. The guest pianist rose to the occasion again and again in swirling crescendos that faded into the musical equivalent of moonlight. As the melody line swelled, it was Nicolas's arms spread in appeal to the violins and piano that caught Carolyn's imagination. Tension and energy seemed to beat from baton to musician and back again. Unbelievably, this performance outdid the previous night's. Surely Alison would love classical music if she heard Nicolas Frost bring it to life. She wished Alison were there.

Nicolas Frost virtually ran from the stage, returning a few moments later to acknowledge the applause and bring the musicians to their feet. A hearty handshake was shared with the pianist and then all bowed again and Nicolas followed the pianist from the stage. Carolyn's box was opposite the musician's entrance and through the backstage shadows she could see the pianist and Nicolas gesturing and shaking hands enthusiastically.

The musicians began returning. Carolyn breathed in deeply as a bass practiced the low melody line of *Seigfried's Funeral March*. The Wagner was next.

Usually by the time Nick reached the top of the runway to the podium her mind was blank except for the music to come. But across the stage, by mere chance, she caught a glimpse of Carolyn Vincense. She was no longer pale as she had been in Paris — her face was aglow with pleasure, pleasure Nick knew somehow she herself had wrought. Giving pleasure to another woman – Nick clenched her hands and ruthlessly drove the idea from her mind. She touched the baton and everything slipped away. Her mind went blank. Her vision dimmed and the silence in her mind grew. She gathered herself and raised the baton, knowing the emptiness in her mind would be filled little by little as she summoned each instrument into its place.

This is why I live as I do.

The music would fill her. The Wagner arrangement she had created filled her own inner silence — she lived through the moments of music. She wasn't the conductor, she was the instrument, and the music stroked every tendon, pressed every nerve.

And she soared.

Carolyn was applauding madly when Nicolas returned to the stage for the fourth time. That arrangement should be recorded – Wagner in Germany, maybe that had something to do with the way the music had seized her imagination, calling forth images of scented gardens and moon-drenched nights, sweeping away rationality.

Nicolas shook hands with the concertmaster and turned again to the audience, bowing. From the side view of the box, Carolyn saw the unbelievable — a full smile that transformed the angularity of Nicolas's face to soft planes. There was something familiar about Nicolas with that smile, but it was gone in a flash.

As the boxes emptied, Carolyn went around backstage and gave her name to the porter, who let her pass. She murmured, *"Schuldigung Sie mir, pardonnez moi, s'cuze,"* as she forged her way through the crowded hallway. When she finally reached the open door of the conductor's dressing room she hesitated. No doubt there were some famous people in there and, for a long moment, Carolyn felt very much like an ordinary woman from Sacramento, California, and she didn't know what on earth she was doing outside a conductor's dressing room.

She heard Oscar's voice then, and her own self-confidence reasserted itself. She was, after all, a successful writer, and she could always talk to Oscar. She squared her shoulders, pretended she had Alison's confidence, and went inside. Oscar saw her immediately.

"Carolyn, how lovely. Nicolas said you would be in attendance this evening. What did you think?" Oscar's expression was light and joyful, as if the music had washed away the sorrow of the afternoon.

"I'm no critic so I don't have the words to describe it. But I thought the top of my head would come off."

Oscar smiled. "Very apt — that's what I thought as well. Now you must tell me where you would like to go tomorrow."

Carolyn rattled off her list, laughing when Oscar rolled his eyes at the most obvious tourist attractions.

"Perhaps I can talk you out of those over dinner after this crowd leaves. Something small and light to top off the day in a civilized manner," Oscar said.

"Uh, I'm already tied up," Carolyn said. Now she felt awkward. Obviously Nicolas hadn't told Oscar about dinner, which meant that Nicolas hadn't intended Oscar to join them, which meant — oh my God — it was a date. She had agreed to a date with a man she didn't even like.

"But of course you are," Oscar said, "and it makes absolute sense that you would be dining out with someone other than an old, crusty music critic."

"You aren't old and crusty," Carolyn protested. "It's just that Nicolas invited me out when he offered the box seat."

"Really?" Oscar exclaimed. His eyes narrowed and something told Carolyn he wasn't pleased. "Come," he said abruptly, "you must meet everyone."

Nick mopped the back of her neck as she tried to find a word or two in her scattered German to express herself to the guest pianist. She wanted to tell Heinrich how wonderful he had been. It had been an exhilarating performance — even more so than last night's. Oh, everything was worth it.

She turned from the pianist as Oscar interrupted them, smoothly introducing Carolyn Vincense. She immediately knew why she had asked Carolyn to dinner – how could she have forgotten those blue eyes? She glanced at Oscar and caught the tail end of a disapproving glare — Oscar definitely looked 'narked. Nick guessed he'd found out about the dinner invitation. Okay, she hadn't realized the extent to which Oscar liked Carolyn — an extremely rare occurrence — so it looked as if she would have to abandon the public relations plan she'd been considering. She would be nice to Carolyn Vincense. No more than nice. She didn't attribute any motive other than pleasing Oscar to her change of motives and plans. It would be wonderful to relax over dinner someplace quiet instead of playing head games in Munich's equivalent of the Savoy. They could just have a friendly, simple dinner.

Oscar continued introducing Carolyn to the other people crowded into the dressing room, announcing her name with the gravity he usually reserved for royalty and adding the imposing information that she was a successful writer. Nick envied Carolyn's fluent German. It sounded perfect. When Oscar gravitated Carolyn back toward them Nick found herself asking for a favor.

"I want to tell Heinrich how masterful his Rachmaninoff was but the only language we really have in common is music," Nick said. "Of course I know German musical terms, and a little conversation, but I'd like to be clear. Would you translate for me?"

She watched a faint blush climb Carolyn's cheeks as she nodded. "Of course."

"Please say that his grasp of the cadenzas exceeds any I have conducted —" Nick broke off when Carolyn put her hand on Nick's sleeve and began to translate. She squeezed Nick's arm as she paused. "And while some of the other musicians may not agree with us, the primary themes should give way ..." Nick went into minute detail, pausing each time Carolyn squeezed her arm. She was finally able to express herself to the pianist who shared a very sympathetic view of Rachmaninoff.

She heard the word *prächtig,* magnificent, which had been one of the last words she'd said. Heinrich then spoke volubly, stopping only when Carolyn put her hand on his arm, as she had Nick's, to make him pause. Nick's arm felt warm where Carolyn's hand had been.

"He says that he is honored to have been conducted by you. A crime, what's a crime, oh – it will be a crime if your Wagner arrangement is not recorded soon. I quite agree," Carolyn said. Her eyes were piercing Nick with a focused blue gaze of concentration. "Perhaps when you are ... at your zenith and recording the Rachmaninoff for posterity you will remember him ..." Heinrich bowed slightly and then they were distracted by new arrivals. Somehow it seemed quite natural when Carolyn continued to translate for Nick. How had she survived without the services of a translator?

After a few minutes Oscar stepped in and the conversation switched to English as Oscar guided the discussion of the night's music, deftly pointing out the finest moments of the performance in such a way as to make them occur to the critic as his own original thoughts. Nick was sure the review would reflect each of Oscar's points. The critic left satisfied, the room at last quieted down. Nick found herself only half listening to the prattle of the first violinist, who was sure he was God's gift to music. His technique was excellent but he had the musical soul of a turnip.

Nick felt the adrenaline subside and decided dinner was moving up on the priority list. The room was emptying and she caught Carolyn's attention. "How about dinner? You've earned it."

"I didn't think I'd be hungry this late at night, but I am," Carolyn said. "I'm ready whenever you are."

"Let me change and we'll go." Nick stepped into the anteroom but not before she caught another of Oscar's disapproving glares. Carolyn was in safe hands, Nick wanted to tell him. She made sure the door was firmly locked, then removed her shirt. She looked at the binding layers of gauze in the mirror. She wanted to take them off and present herself to Carolyn as a woman. That realization made her stomach do a slow flip-flop. Carolyn was, with almost one hundred percent surety, going out with Nick because she thought Nick was a man. It was a date. So how could she present herself to Carolyn as a woman and hope for a flicker of interest? She wanted Carolyn's company, but she would have to stay a man to have it.

5

Crescendo

Despite her sudden eagerness for a quiet dinner, Nick didn't mean to enjoy herself — not this much anyway. Carolyn was unlike most of the people she met these days. She was quiet and lovely in an unexotic way — more Brahms than Stravinsky. It didn't matter that the image of robins' eggs was corny, Carolyn Vincense's eyes were precisely that shade of blue. After the company of violinists and concertmasters, Carolyn's presence was restful and undemanding; once Carolyn relaxed a little, Nick found talking to her very easy.

Their sautéed scampi appetizers were delivered quickly and Nick poured a glass of champagne for each of them. She described life in London and, over a second glass of champagne, asked about life in America — everything she'd heard about California made it out to be a paradise. She longed to see the gay districts of San Francisco where men were reputed to walk openly hand in hand. Where women kissed on street corners and gathered in bookstores filled with literature for gays and lesbians and staged "kiss-ins" for tourists so the whole world would get the idea that gay people were everywhere. Even in Paris she had seen nothing so blatant. Of course Carolyn mentioned nothing about gays.

The vision of such freedom and the champagne bubbles went to her head as she listened, and then she suddenly drifted away. She stepped outside her body, saw herself nodding in response to Carolyn. Except the Nick at the table was dressed in a white lace tuxedo, the front of which swelled in two key places. As Nick watched her fantasy play out, she saw herself reach out and take Carolyn's hand.

Oh stop it, she told herself. Pay attention to what she's saying. She had another sip of the cool champagne, but it was too late. She was obsessed with imagining the texture of Carolyn's skin.

You are holding her hand. You feel it tremble in your grasp. She doesn't resist as you draw her to her feet, encircle her waist, tip her head back and drink deeply from that gentle mouth.

Nick could hear white lace whispering against Carolyn's skin as she imagined spreading Carolyn over the tablecloth. *You are alone with her, in this crowded restaurant, alone with her as you possess her mouth. Her whispers are for you as your hand guides her, leads her, possesses her. You listen and kiss her again, leading her along the path to climax, to the final surge of violins.*

You know she is helpless, you control her completely. She is hanging on your every caress, murmuring her pleasure as you bare her body, just for you, your lace against the soft white clouds of her breasts.

"Nick," she will breathe. "Nick?"

"Hmm? — Oh, sorry," Nick mumbled. Oh bother. What was she thinking, having a fantasy like that in a public place about a woman who thought she was dating a man? She had never had this problem before. "I was daydreaming. The champagne seems particularly potent."

"I think our entrees are on their way. You must be tired," Carolyn said.

"The adrenaline is wearing off." Liar! Nick could feel her heart pounding. "I remember one time when I actually passed out after a performance, a long, long time ago." She stopped, realizing she had been about to share a reminiscence from her conservatory days. The days when she'd been a woman. But she was still a woman. Signals from influential parts of her lower body were reminding her that she was most definitely a woman. Oh bother.

"It's hard to picture you so vulnerable," Carolyn said.

"I was, once." She tried to dampen her smile but it wouldn't turn off. "So what brings you to Europe? Oscar said you're on holiday."

"Well, it was time for an adventure," Carolyn said.

"How fortunate that you can indulge yourself," she observed.

"Yes, isn't it!" A happy blow accompanied those words. "My books were picked up for foreign distribution and I'm traveling on an advance. Next is Amsterdam, then Madrid for sun, Salzburg for Mozart, and Rome for *la dolce vita*. When I get back to Sacramento it will be back to a much more ordinary life, and back to a budget again."

"You said you were a writer, but you didn't say successful. Musicians and writers are a lot alike," Nick said. "Being able to live off our creations is the exception, not the rule."

"I feel very, very lucky. I write romantic fiction and it seems to keep selling."

Oh bloody hell, she's an overwrought romantic. A heterosexual romantic. She's too nice to use for press fodder, and it looks like she's too impressionable. "Why do you think it sells?" As if that makes a difference to my fantasies, Nick thought. *A fine mess I've got myself in.*

"As a genre it gets no respect — but fortunately I don't write for critics, I write for women. Carly Vincent likes to reinforce the principle that no woman should have to choose less than the best for herself."

"And how does Carolyn Vincense feel about that?"

Carolyn's intense expression shifted abruptly to chagrin. "Well, Carolyn Vincense must believe it too." She cleared her throat and sipped at her champagne. "I was married for two whole weeks. It was a holiday romance. And when it was obvious it had been a mistake I ... deleted it, like a chapter I decided was going the wrong direction for a book. Funny, I've never seen it that clearly before. I guess talking about it helps."

Nick suddenly felt out of her depth. "I'm not exactly known for my prowess as a lonely-hearts advisor," she said in a joking tone. "In fact, I've been called a cold fish on more than one occasion."

"You come across that way, but I can't help but think it's deliberate."

Nick was surprised at Carolyn's sudden frankness. Her cheeks were brushed with delicate color — maybe the champagne was having an effect? "Why would it be deliberate?"

"The music betrays you." Carolyn smiled, then looked up at Nick through her lashes. The look was not so much coy as shy. "I think I've got your number."

Nick choked on a swallow. Carolyn couldn't have guessed so easily what Nick spent so much energy concealing. The waiter suddenly appeared with their entrees and after the fuss of rearranging the dishes and commenting on the appearance of the food, Nick said as casually as she could manage, "What number is that?"

"You have a long road ahead of you and you can't afford to slow down," Carolyn said. "So you pour all your emotional qualities into the music. That Mozart in Paris, for instance. You found just the right emotional content to save it from sounding like a sewing machine, and restrained it before it got to Muzak level."

"Thank you," Nick said, genuinely gratified. "Words *are* your trade, obviously. That was very succinct, and, I must say, extremely accurate." She smiled at her boast, and decided Carolyn was not hinting that she'd guessed Nick was a woman. It was just a false alarm.

"Thank *you*," Carolyn said, with a mocking nod.

They concentrated on their meals for a while. Carolyn's beef curry looked delectable but Nick was entirely satisfied with her coq au vin. A distracted expression crossed Carolyn's face.

"Ha'penny for your thoughts," Nick said.

"Oh. Well, I was just thinking that there's something I really must tell you. It's a confession – not the sort of thing a person admits to someone like you, at least not right away."

Nick's pulse was racing again. What on earth was Carolyn leading up to? "If you feel you must ..." Nick said. She had no idea what to expect.

"I — I have to confess that – well," Carolyn looked down at her plate and muttered quickly, "I really, *really* like Barry Manilow." The words were followed with a grin of impish delight as Nick nearly choked again.

"Well ... that's the last thing I thought you would say," Nick said after she'd swallowed some water to clear her throat. "I hardly expected it from a woman of your intelligence."

"Don't forget I'm a romance writer. I have extremely trashy impulses at times. He's underrated as a musician." They argued all the way through dinner about popular culture versus the higher arts. Nick ended up confessing that she liked American football and, like Bernstein, couldn't resist Tina Turner.

When they had finished their lime sorbets, Nick found herself saying, "It's very welcome to talk to someone who isn't a part of *serious* music."

"Or advances and sales figures and – the hundred tedious things that romance writers talk about at conventions. That's work for me and I like it when I'm there, but – well, this is welcome, as you say." Carolyn stared down at her empty sorbet glass. "Nick, I'm not flirting," she said abruptly. She looked up, piercing Nick with the gaze from her robin's eggs-eyes. "I'm not."

Nick realized her heartbeat was doing a tarantella. God, if this wasn't flirting then heaven only knew how dangerous Carolyn could be when she did flirt. "I know. I take your honesty as a sincere compliment from – someone who doesn't like me much." What would she say to that? Nick held her breath.

"I'm getting over my first impression. After all, I'm not throwing up at the moment." Carolyn laughed.

Nick hid her shudder. She felt as if she were on the French railway, racing headlong into the unknown. "Carolyn," she said, stifling a hiccup, "can I ask a favor of you?" Carolyn didn't answer but looked at her hesitantly. After a moment, Nick went on. "I'm in Brussels for almost a week, but right in the middle of my stay I have a lecture in The Hague. It takes just the morning, then I fly back to Brussels late in the evening. Would you – like to spend the day with me in The Hague? Could we be ... friends? Friends who sightsee and have dinner together?"

Carolyn lowered her gaze, then said, "That

sounds perfect to me. I had been planning to take the rail down the coast to The Hague and then zip over to Delft to buy some pottery for my sister-in-law. I hope that's not too prosaic. It's all I'm looking for." They stared at each other for a few moments, then Nick raised her glass and they solemnly toasted friendship.

Nick couldn't remember when she had felt so comfortable and so uncomfortable at the same time. How could she – court a woman who didn't know she wasn't a man? Nick couldn't very well tell her outright especially after she'd said she just wanted to be friends. And what would Oscar say? Oh bother.

They walked the short distance back to the hotel and parted with a wave. Maybe it would be all right, Nick thought. Even if she never found out I'm a woman I could certainly use a few more pleasant dinners in Carolyn's company.

Her blood pressure felt as if it had dropped fifty points — even though her heartbeat was still at tarantella tempo. But deep down, under her boxer shorts, Nick knew she was hoping for more than dinner. And that hope, if she wasn't careful, would betray her secret.

♥

"Get your bags, miss?" Carolyn jumped, startled by the British voice, not expecting it in a rail transfer station in downtown Amsterdam. She pushed her hair out of her eyes but the rain-laden wind whipped it back across her forehead again.

"Yes, please, and a cab." The porter was no more than a boy, Carolyn thought, and she smiled at his antics while he hailed a cab and loaded her suitcases into it. As she tipped him, the watery sun suddenly cast an odd shadow across her helper's face and Carolyn realized that He was a She. The girl winked and thanked her, and Carolyn thought, "More power to her."

She directed the driver to her hotel and sat back, looking at the Dutch buildings and people around her. While she unpacked she tried not to miss the companionship she'd had with Oscar only that morning. Munich had been great fun and Oscar had been pleased by her eager absorption of his opinions. When she asked about Nick, however, he had adroitly changed the subject. She wondered why her innocent dinner with Nick had bothered Oscar, but supposed that he felt it might undercut Nick's concentration. She had felt secretive for not mentioning her arrangement to see Nick in The Hague later in the week, but then again, telling Oscar was Nick's business, not hers.

She examined a note from the tour company offering her a seat on a bus going to a country market, but Carolyn rejected the idea. She was doing quite well all by herself. The next morning she set out in her most comfortable walking shoes, warm wool slacks and, in British parlance, a stout anorak. Her first stop was a *banketbakkerij* where she bought some deliciously sinful honey buns. Happily sticky, she licked her fingers and began her tour of the Rijksmuseum.

Rembrandt and Vermeer masterpieces greeted her. She'd come to Amsterdam for the Flemish and Dutch masters, and she lost herself in the paintings, studying the black backgrounds that suggested capes and gloves and walls, masterful tricks of light. At lunch she devoured an *uitsmijter* with thick slices of cheese made in Gouda, a few kilometers away. In the afternoon she hunted down a diamond-cutting demonstration.

The next few days were similar. She spent nearly a day at the Van Gogh Museum. What a violent passion for life – she felt bludgeoned by the color and radiance of the paintings. She tried to express the beauty of them in another five postcards to Alison, but her senses were overloaded with all the sights and sounds. A lousy photographer, she bought a good many postcards for herself, too, to remind her of the sun-streaked gothic buildings and intricately carved bridges spanning the canals. There was no such thing as an ordinary bridge in the entire city.

The night before she was going to take the train to Den Haag, she made her way to the Concertgebouw for her Dutch orchestra treat. She studied her program, learning that the night's performance of Mozart, Dvorak and Debussy was the finale of the Amsterdam concert season. The acoustics of the famed concert hall were everything the travel guide had promised – but she still felt a little let down by the music. It was certainly equal to any she might have expected. The conductor was very good, but not – brilliant.

That conclusion aggravated her. She was overly critical, having been spoiled by the talent of Nicolas Frost. She wished she'd never agreed to go to The Hague tomorrow — she'd be sorry, she just knew it. Where was her head?

But in the morning, ensconced in a warm cabin with six other passengers, she forgot her worries.

The train's rhythm was soothing, and as they sped through the drizzle falling from high clouds, she watched the watery sunlight add picturesque shadows to flat fields of sprouting hay. She had a stilted conversation with another passenger after she exclaimed over the beauty of a tulip field in full bloom. Before she knew it, the man — wearing a wedding ring, no less — had offered to show her around The Hague and even alluded to a friend's apartment where they could have a picnic lunch. Carolyn lapsed into uncomprehending English at that point, and wondered why men thought sex was for the asking. Linda had warned her a woman traveling alone was considered fair game in Europe, but it rankled nonetheless. Just because men thought it so didn't make it fair.

She was glad to leave the train when it pulled into the station. It was just after ten and she had enough time to hurry through the Mauritshuis to see Rembrandt's *Anatomy Lesson of Dr. Tulip* and then rush to the university. She waited almost half an hour on the corner Nick had specified and was beginning to doubt her location when she became aware of another umbrella over her own.

"My apologies," Nick said. Carolyn couldn't tell if the voice was husky from the weather or from speaking all morning. "Well, I'm sure you have a detailed agenda for the day, so where first?"

By dinner time, finally driven indoors by increasingly heavy rain, Carolyn couldn't remember why she had thought Nick a boor. The restaurant was family-owned and filled with the aroma of fresh-baked bread. They shook water off their coats and surrendered them to be dried before a roaring fire. Carolyn found herself ordering hard cider and fondue for two without consulting Nick, and then was surprised by the indulgent smile Nick directed at her.

"What's so funny?"

"You've been ordering me around all day. It's a refreshing change. You've probably taken a hundred points off my blood pressure and added a year to my life."

"Well, there's something to be said for not being in control one hundred percent of the time. Besides, I'm starving. No time to dither over a menu."

"If you were home what would you be having?" Nick leaned back in the chair, one hand sweeping back wet hair that threatened to curl and fall forward on her forehead.

"Probably two all beef patties, special sauce, lettuce, cheese, pickles, onions on a sesame seed bun," she said. At Nick's look of incomprehension, Carolyn elaborated. "The Golden Arches, MacDonald's, you know? My best friend, Alison, her favorite fast-food meal is a Big Mac with fries dipped in strawberry shake."

Nick shuddered. "Sounds revolting."

"It is. But right now I'd kill for a Pop-Tart. All that walking." She gratefully sipped the ice-cold hard cider their server delivered with a curtsy. The kick burned her throat and she coughed. "Whoa – this stuff is more than hard."

Nick sipped and nodded. "Every once in a while during the summer the home-crushed cider at the orphanage would turn. Mother Superior kept that for her private stock."

"You really are an orphan?"

"Really and truly," Nick answered. Again, one hand smoothed the curling hair back, this time more insistently.

The firelight brought softness to Nick's face. Carolyn found herself studying the features she knew could be cold and hard. The fondue was spicy with aged cheeses and Nick lost even more dignity when a cube of cheese-smothered bread snaked down her sober charcoal tie. Nick stared down at it with a frown and then, sighing, removed the tie.

"Ties are an incredible pain."

"Oh complain, complain." The hard cider was sending lovely warm sparkles through her toes and fingers. "A little strip of fabric less than two inches wide. You have no idea what pain is — try wearing pantyhose for a day and then we'll talk about discomfort. The only good thing about pantyhose is the wonderful relief you feel when you take them off." She smiled. "It's a pleasure unique to the female of the species." To her amazement, she saw a sudden flush of color rise in Nick's cheeks. One of the candles on the table flared for a moment, and the slant of light illuminated Nick's pale skin, stained by patches of red at the cheeks and forehead. Nick's hair was drying to a soft, curly fuzz.

Carolyn was sure of it — Nick was blushing. The color changed the angular and austere face completely as Nick stared intently at the cider goblets. Carolyn could almost see the surge of will that grappled with some powerful emotion.

The server returned to ask if they'd decided on a main course. The hard cider made Carolyn's mind behave oddly, as if her synapses were backfiring valves in an engine. She let Nick select the entree and stared at Nick's profile, and her mind's eye colored it again with the vulnerable and open blush.

Carolyn bit back a gasp. *How could I have missed it? Because, like the rest of the world, I saw what Nicolas wanted me to see. But I must be right — Nick is a woman.*

Carolyn recognized an immense wave of relief. So this was why she felt entirely comfortable with Nick. Nick was a *woman*; it was natural to be able to talk with a woman as a friend. But something else about Nick was incredibly attractive, and Carolyn felt faint with new, contradictory emotions. She remembered the sensation that had swept through her when she'd seen the two women in the Louvre. Hilary and Jane — the devotion they had showed each other had come to mind again and again.

What will I tell Alison? This new thought blazed through Carolyn's backfiring brain. *Alison* — in less than a heartbeat Carolyn reevaluated fifteen years of close friendship. Had it been attraction she'd felt for her all these years? *How long have I been wanting something more?* She felt as if she'd spent the first thirty years of her life wrapped in cotton. Someone should have told her, given her a test — it would have saved her so much wasted anguish. She'd never have married, never regretted it, never wondered. *Why didn't I know?* The vague feelings of attraction were pulsingly concrete now, because Nick was a woman.

Which means I'm ... no, no I'm not! Carolyn wanted to run to someplace where she wouldn't be alone with herself. She watched Nick nod, and noticed for the first time the soft and downy hair fuzzing the back of Nick's neck.

Nick couldn't know how she felt. If Nick realized Carolyn knew she was a woman, and that Carolyn was fiercely attracted to Nick, then Nick would know ... would know what Carolyn hadn't known until this moment.

"Carolyn? You're white as a sheet." Nick's cool voice cut into Carolyn's thoughts.

Her mind was a maelstrom. "No, I'm fine. I'm ... just suddenly very tired." He — no, *she*, — had managed a near impossible game, in a struggle for the recognition of talent. She knew of many romance writers who wrote other genres under masculine pseudonyms, but Nick was living it, every day. Like George Sand and Gertrude Stein ... many well-known women had worn men's clothing. I can't let her know I know, Carolyn told herself. She has kept her secret for years. I'll just go on sharing friendship with her.

"Well, I've ordered us a balanced meal and then I'm afraid I'll have to hurry to make my plane."

Carolyn glanced at her watch. "Oh, I hadn't realized it had gotten so late."

Under the guise of pressing time, Carolyn ate her entree in near silence, hoping she could finish the meal and get Nicolas Frost out of her life before she betrayed her newly discovered secret — and Nick's secret as well. She yearned to ask a million questions ... how long had Nick been posing as a man, and didn't the disguise make romance impossible? Was Oscar her lover? But no, that didn't seem likely. She could tell Nick was studying her as they shrugged into their toasty warm coats again.

Outside the rain caught her by surprise, but she tried to maintain a nonchalant façade as they searched for a taxi stand.

"Are you sure you're up to the train trip back to Amsterdam?" Nick turned in the back seat of the cab to face her directly. Carolyn was glad of the darkness.

"I'm sure. I'm just tired and the trip it's not that far."

"I've had fun," Nick said. "When are you in Salzburg?"

Carolyn had been alternately hoping and dreading this question. They swapped hotel names since their itineraries overlapped. Carolyn's heart was beating like the final thirty seconds of Ravel's *Bolero* when they pulled up to the train station. She got out of the cab, promising to call Nick in Salzburg, more than a week in the future.

"Carolyn," Nick called, after she had gone a few steps. She turned — Nick was getting out of the cab.

"You'll get wet." She hurried back to the cab.

"I don't mind," Nick said. "I just wanted ... to tell you how much today meant to me. I don't often get to let my hair down, so to speak."

Carolyn bit her lower lip. "It was my pleasure. Friendship, we toasted friendship, remember?"

"I remember," Nick said softly. Carolyn didn't move as Nick bent slowly. Their lips pressed long enough for Carolyn to register how warm Nick's felt against hers, and then Nick was sliding into the dark recesses of the cab. "See you in Salzburg," Nick said before the door shut between them.

She sat on the brightly lit train in a daze, glad

of its high speed taking her as far away from Nicolas Frost as she could get. It seemed no time before she was rushing through Schipol Airport, and then headed for Amsterdam, then in her hotel room. The sensation of Nick's lips on hers still lingered. She stared at herself in the mirror, searching for some sign of difference. No difference – except the slight shudder as she recalled the way another woman's lips had felt on her own.

Nick ... the attraction was no longer vague. She wanted to see Nick's body in its true form. She groaned again. Her own body was a flame.

She took a bath, the water as hot as she could stand it, and her hands explored her body. She caressed her calves, wondering if other women's calves felt muscular and yet soft. Her hands studied the ridges of her ribs, then explored slowly and thoroughly the yielding gentleness of her breasts. To touch another woman like this ... she slid down into the soapy water, her skin on fire, her mind burning with images of Alison, Samantha, Linda, Rochelle — every woman she knew. And now Nick. She slipped her hands between her legs. Did Nick feel like this?

She rose from the water at last, shivering with emotions she was only beginning to articulate. She burrowed under the sheets, trying to hide, but the word persisted in her head, a word she never thought she'd apply to herself. *Lesbian,* an inner voice whispered.

6

Intermezzo

Alison surreptitiously examined the mail Devon
was sorting. There were three postcards which Devon
read before passing them on with his usual snide
remarks. But no sign of any airmail envelopes. It did
not bode well that the last thing Carolyn had
written about was some Oscar person and the
conductor. And what right do I have to wonder what
she's doing, Alison asked herself. I'm not exactly

keeping myself . . . chaste . . . for her. What she was doing with Sam was anything but chaste.

"You're going to be late," Devon said. "Hadn't you better change?"

"Thanks for the reminder," Alison said. She shut the door to her office and stripped off her suit and hose. Now that the mail had finally arrived there was no reason to hang around. She stepped into comfortable jeans, pulled on sweat socks and worn tennis shoes and yanked a lightweight sweatshirt over her head. The clothes greeted her like old friends. The first practice of the season was always great.

Buddies not seen since last September waved greetings as she got out of her car. Sam left the group she'd been standing with and met Alison halfway to the field. "Ain't it grand to be back on green grass?"

"I wouldn't mind being on my back in green grass, not at all."

Sam swatted her, but her nose crinkled in a pleased way. "That's not what I said. But I'd be willing to oblige later."

"Promises, promises."

"Hey, break it up, you two." The team captain threw baseball gloves at them. "No flirting before the game."

"Flirting is only allowed during innings six and nine," someone else said. There was a shared groan.

Within a few hours, out in right field again, Alison felt back in shape and at ease. It was obvious that her weak spot at the plate was still a slider breaking inside. Sam batted terrifically as usual, and

Alison was surprised to find herself a little weak in the knees as she watched Sam running for first, trying to beat the throw. She was easily the sexiest woman on the playing field and Alison didn't know why it had taken her so long to notice. Sam slid and slapped the bag just like Ricky Henderson. She stood up, beating dust off the California Raisins adorning her T-shirt. Alison's knees became downright watery as she considered kissing Sam's raisins. It didn't help that as Sam stood on first she sent smoldering glances Alison's way between pitches.

Alison nodded as if hypnotized when Sam suggested going back to her place. They got in the van, not speaking, and once inside Sam's apartment Alison reached for Sam. Her nostrils filled with the smell of sweat and dust and she realized she'd never noticed how erotic it was.

"Uh, I was going to suggest a shower," Sam said.

Alison slid slowly to her knees. "Later," she murmured, her hands unbuttoning the fly of Sam's 501s. She pulled Sam's jeans down and rubbed her lips over the thick, tight curls, savoring the tingles the coarse hair brought to her skin. Sam leaned back against the nearest piece of furniture, the back of a sofa, and Alison tipped her head up, mouth burrowing and tongue diving.

"Wait, let me get my balance —" Too late. Before Alison could grab hold Sam went backwards over the sofa and collapsed on the cushions, her legs in the air and feet waving while she giggled.

Alison laughed and wiped her mouth with the back of her hand. With a banshee yell she dove over the sofa after Sam. The wrestling match that followed was entirely satisfactory, to Alison's mind, as the goal seemed to be relieving each other of unnecessary clothing. She had no idea how she ended up under the coffee table but all she had to worry about was smacking the back of her head on it.

"You pick interesting places to make love," Alison said later. "I hope you treated those rocker cushions with some sort of moisture repellent."

Sam was on the floor on her back staring at the ceiling. "It will add a certain something to the ambience of this room." She focused on Alison's face. "You're pretty good, you know that?"

"So are you."

"Heard from Carolyn lately?"

Alison looked sharply at Sam. "Why do you ask that now?"

"Because you've just answered the real question. Don't worry. I can wait." She rolled over onto her stomach in a flash of long legs and tumbled hair.

"Sam ..." Alison's protest about using Sam and fairness and what wasn't right and what would be the correct thing to do died on her lips as Sam nibbled at her kneecaps.

"I hate the fact that she's alone in Europe," Alison said.

Sam rolled out of the jumble of sheets and blankets and regarded Alison with a steady gaze. "Then why don't you go after her?"

"I'm chicken." Alison gathered an armful of blanket and rested her head on it.

"Look, Ally, don't think I'm being altruistic about this. I can tell you'll never be free to really be with me until you're free of her. I've been in love with you for quite a while and I didn't know why you never noticed. I thought it was racial – I mean, you made a good friend, but maybe you didn't like black women in bed, I didn't know. Well, you obviously do like black women in bed, at least this black woman." Sam took a deep breath.

"I don't know why we hadn't –" Alison let her voice trail away. She wanted to be honest. "If I didn't notice how gorgeous you were because you're black, then I'm not too proud of myself."

Sam spoke pensively. "Maybe that has something to do with it, but you haven't been with anyone else on the team — not that I know of." At Alison's shake of the head, she continued, "I think your mind is more attached to Carolyn than you think."

"I haven't exactly been celibate since I fell in love with her."

"Thank God. You have a nice technique." She looked away from Alison. "Look, if I'm going to lose you to her then I'd rather it was sooner than later. While what you do to me is very pleasant, I'm not willing to live a half-life for it. I hold myself in too much esteem for that."

A *half-life*. "Is that what you think I'm doing with Carolyn?"

"Only you know that," Sam said. "I just know that I've never made a woman c-r-y twice."

"How do you know white women don't cry afterwards?" Alison hadn't thought Sam had noticed while they were in the shower. Touching Sam had been so sweet and yet she had wanted to weep.

"Give me a little credit," Sam said.

"Maybe I'm cracking up."

"Well, either go after Carolyn or see a therapist," Sam snapped. Then she sighed. "Sorry, I thought I could be a big girl about this. I love you, Ally. I thought I could do this until I made you love me back, but I was wrong. Don't take this the wrong way, but I think you should get dressed now."

In a daze, Alison retrieved her clothes from the various parts of the living room. She went back to the bedroom and watched Sam from the doorway. "You're being awfully good to me."

"I play to w-i-n," Sam said, with a smile. She tugged her hair back and expertly wrapped a bandeau around it. "Now you know what you're missing."

Alison didn't drive straight home after Sam dropped her back at the practice field. She drove aimlessly, trying to think clearly. Sam had probably saved her a fortune in therapy, but she still had a lot to think about. She couldn't just go after Carolyn, could she? If she told Carolyn how she felt ... the worst that could happen was that they would only have Carly Vincent in common and that would drive Alison mad with irony.

She took an offramp near midtown and drove down G Street with purpose. Enough waiting, she told herself. If you lose Carolyn, Sam will be there to fill the gap. And she could get used to having Sam in her life. She just needed to be free. As she parallel-parked, Alison caught sight of herself in the rear view mirror and laughed. Carolyn didn't even know she had a hold of Alison. And while she could be quite happy with Sam, it would only be if she knew Carolyn would never love her.

She took a deep breath and looked at the door to the travel agency. Linda owed her a favor or two. She could find out exactly when Carolyn would be where. *It will be easy,* an inner voice whispered. *She's probably lonely by now. She'll be glad to see you.*

"Nah!" Alison spoke for the benefit of the woman in the mirror, who looked far too hopeful.

♥

Carolyn's first day in Madrid was spent in the bazaars in La Gran Via shopping for yet more presents to take home with her. Her two nephews were easy, and she found a pair of long silver earrings that would look great dangling from Alison's pale earlobes. She'd never seen a double-sided axe on an earring, but the work was delicately detailed, and Carolyn would suggest that the next time a publisher got nasty Alison could hack the representative into little bits.

The shopkeeper had given Carolyn a warm, toothy smile, with a flash of something in her eyes that made Carolyn blush. She'd asked, after Carolyn had spoken to her in passable Spanish, if Carolyn was an American companion, *compañera,* and at Carolyn's blank stare, elaborated by asking if she were a tortilla-maker, a *tortillera,* which was quite possibly the oddest question anyone had ever asked her. Carolyn had mumbled a vague response about tortillas being her favorite food and escaped, her heart beating high up in her throat.

The symphony that marked the middle of her stay was more informal than any of the ones she'd seen to date. Even the music seemed willing to go with the flow — why sweat and hurry? It floated around her ears in soothing eddies of sound. The selections honored Spanish and Portuguese composers, concluding with a whimsical and fresh series from *Carmen*.

The second day she spent at the Museo Cerralbo and Museo del Prado. In Amsterdam she'd feasted on Rembrandt; here she feasted on Valasquez and El Greco. She walked past a bullring throbbing with yells of *"Olé "* [but the very idea of attending made her queasy. She'd read Hemingway and that was as close as she was going to get. She had a feeling the real thing was a lot less romantic than Hemingway's descriptions.]

At siesta she sat in her room to write another letter to Alison — she was itching with the need to say something, to get things out in the open. She'd always been able to write each letter completely through, without second-guessing herself. But she had to tell Alison the truth.

Dear Alison:
I've discovered something new about myself —
The second draft was even less satisfactory.
Dearest Alison:
I've —
The third draft had only the date on it for the longest time, and then Carolyn realized siesta was over. She wandered back to La Gran Via where the

merchants were spreading out their wares again. She had a tall frosted lime concoction at a cafe, then she wandered back to her room and ordered something similar from room service. The tequila gave her courage.

Dear Alison:

I'm having a wonderful time and wishing you were here. The pace of life in Madrid would do you good. Everything is mañana, tomorrow is soon enough. She prattled on for a while about Madrid and the museums and then finished with:

Ally, there's something I'm not telling you and it's quite delicate. I'll tell you when I see you. You're my best friend, and if you stop caring for me I don't know what I'll do, but what I have to say could change everything. As always,

Carolyn

♥

Linda confirmed that Alison could, by leaving within forty-eight hours, meet up with Carolyn on her first night in Rome. There was no way she'd catch her in Salzburg. Alison kept a firm grip on the letter. She knew it shouldn't change the promises she'd made herself about being cured of Carolyn, but it did. She'd read it, and between its lines, at least twenty times. Maybe she was jumping to the biggest conclusion of all time, but she preferred to think of it as a leap of faith.

♥

The Salzburg Mozart Festival was in full swing when Nick stepped from her plane. The air was still crisp — though not frigid, as it had been in Oslo — and she was glad for her extra padding.

There were signs of festival everywhere in the central hotel district. After they had checked in and unpacked, Oscar had pleaded fatigue, leaving Nick biting her tongue with everything she wanted to say to him. Oscar, by his very reticence, demonstrated he knew something was amiss. How could she tell him she'd kissed Carolyn Vincense? How could she say she'd been dying a little each day until she saw Carolyn because she wanted to kiss Carolyn again? She knew she was running headlong down a path to ruin. She knew Oscar would try to talk her out of it. But when it came to Carolyn she found she had no control whatsoever. How was she going to achieve anything remotely satisfying with Carolyn? Just being friends wasn't at all fulfilling.

She knew Salzburg as well as the Mozart *Requiem* she was conducting in Dokm, the Great Cathedral. Rehearsals for the Sunday performance started first thing tomorrow, and doubled up her schedule — she also had rehearsals for the Salzburg Philharmonic performance. She wouldn't have a chance to visit old stomping grounds again.

She listened to the Glockenspiel and her thoughts wandered. The last time she had heard the rich, clear tones she had been a woman. She clenched her hands into fists. Bloody hell, she was *still* a woman. She still loved her vagina and clitoris and breasts. And she loved women. In this garb, to love women should be natural and easy. Dressed as a man she could start up flirtatious conversation with any woman she saw and be thought completely natural. Dressed as a man she could be a pest, make insulting comments and send drinks to women's tables and be thought completely natural. Dressed as a man she could look at the smorgasbord of women around her, pick one out and expect the woman to do whatever she liked, and most people would say that was completely natural. But if she changed her attire and appeared a woman and she did so much as tell another woman she thought her beautiful, most people would say it was perverted. The clothing was a lie. Underneath was truth.

So how did she want to live? In lies or in truth? The desire for another woman's body was a surging pulse, and the pressing urges of her libido made logical thought very difficult.

She had Schnitzel Cordon Bleu — ham, veal, cheese, dipped in egg and fried ... oh she hadn't had it in such a long time, like something else she could think of. She lusted after all the woman she saw, returned a few smiles and nods of interest. She felt a fraud, suddenly — not the clothing, this time, but because she'd read an article on the plane that Oscar had clipped for her about a woman in America who was conducting an all-woman philharmonic, in addition to traditional orchestral assignments. Nick hoped that brave woman would some day get her due. But because Nick was living a lie, she would most likely get the big break first, even though this woman in America had been conducting for ten years, all the while resurrecting and performing works by woman composers. Nick felt herself to be a complete fraud, and she envied Joann Falletta — the woman in America — from the bottom of her heart. She had always thought her own priorities were in order, but shadows of doubt had caught up with her.

Shadows of doubt and the full spectrum of lust — after two steins of bock she decided she couldn't stop seeing Carolyn. In fact, the two days before Carolyn arrived seemed an eternity, but at least she would be honest about it. She wanted to see Carolyn so she could be a woman with her and God help Nick if Carolyn went running to the nearest newspaper when she found out.

Despite a muzzy head when she went to sleep, she woke refreshed the next morning and ready for rehearsals. She hummed Mozart in honor of his birthplace. Rehearsals were at ten sharp, and she arrived early, wanting some small peace in the Cathedral before the others arrived. She wasn't completely alone, but she sat down in the back and wondered if prayer would do her any good.

Probably not. Prayer, here, wasn't going to do the likes of her any good. Maybe she should make a pilgrimage to Delphi where the Goddess once enlightened the Priestesses of Apollo. Or to Lesbos. Or just inside herself.

She wasn't surprised when Oscar sat down next to her.

"I have something to tell you," she said immediately.

"I think I can guess. You've been walking on air since that lecture in The Hague. I'm perfectly aware of how far The Hague is from Amsterdam." Oscar examined the handle of his walking stick.

"It was a wonderful day. I ... have to try for

more wonderful days. You may think that it'll cost me everything I've worked for, but if I don't try for some peace I'm going to lose it all anyway."

"I have been pretending that your life is simple, but no one should know better than I that it isn't," Oscar said. More performers were assembling.

"She arrives tomorrow," Nick said.

Oscar nodded. Nick rose to greet the choirmaster.

♥

Carolyn had a long list of sights she wanted to see in Salzburg, and she methodically went about her task, checking each one off her list as if she were making an extremely organized trip to the grocery store. She would see everything she wanted, whether Nick called or not. She hoped Nick wouldn't call. She could go on hiding from herself for just a little longer if only she didn't have to confront Nick again. She asked herself, for the thousandth time, why Nick had kissed her. Had Nick thought she expected it? Had Carolyn in some way acted as if she wanted it? Was Nick just trying to keep her cover as a man secure?

The Marionettentheater was performing in the square when Carolyn walked past Mirabell Palace. Carolyn sat among the children, laughing as the puppets butchered *The Magic Flute*. She kept one eye on the clock in the Glockenspiel. She had an appointment at the mineral spas.

Carolyn had never been reluctant about taking her clothes off in gym class. She was modest, but not shy. It had seemed natural to admire other women. When she was twelve it had seemed natural to compare. But as she stood in the changing room for the spa, having made what could only be a leap of faith in the last week, she couldn't stop a blush as she avoided and yet sought out the sight of the other women's bodies. She knew why she looked. She knew why it seemed natural — it was. Her body sent confirmations to her heart — *it's natural, it's good.* Swelling hips, the satin line of thighs — Carolyn turned away, shocked by the surge of erotic energy in her body, only to find other bodies catching her gaze.

She soaked in the steaming water, and knew that the heat inside wouldn't entirely go away when she showered. She laughed to herself. In romantic Paris she had decided, once and for all, that she was frigid. In cool Salzburg she was burning with sexual possibilities. Either there's a lesson there, she told herself, or it's just plain old-fashioned irony.

She had signed up for the all-body massage. The muscular, statuesque woman left almost no part of Carolyn untouched. Carolyn could only hope that the masseuse put Carolyn's perspiration and high color down to the vigor of the massage, and did not attribute it to her blonde hair and Nordic figure. She recalled suddenly how flustered she had felt around Samantha and her dark beauty. How warm – yes, she was definitely entering a warm period. A highly tactile period when everything from the rough towel under her to a silk blouse sent shivers through her body. The flustered thoughts about Samantha recalled similar flustered thoughts about Alison, and then Nick of course came to mind again. She refused to hope for a message when she got back to her hotel.

There were four messages. The last three were marked "urgent."

"How does a gala sound?" Nick's voice was not its usual abrupt tone — much warmer, in fact.

"Well, I've got a concert tonight ... not yours, I'm afraid," Carolyn said as naturally as she could manage. The massage had left her energized and strong.

Nick made a disparaging noise. "Rubbish, I'm sure. Well, maybe you could just drop in and ... that'll give us a chance to compare schedules. I'd love to sight-see with you again. Why don't I leave a ticket to the gala for you at the door and maybe we could slip away and make plans."

"A gala sounds interesting," Carolyn said finally. "Tell me where."

"Schloss Mirabell ... do you know where that is?"

"I walked by it this afternoon. I'd love to see the inside. I'll be there." Well, Carolyn told herself, if she had something to look at and explore, then seeing Nick would probably have less impact on her composure. Right.

A gala called for her best outfit, she decided, which was a raw silk suit in black she had bought on impulse in Madrid. She belted an elegant strand of silver links that Alison had given her around the tunic, and tucked the pants into her calf-height boots. She surveyed herself critically. She hoped she looked cool and aloof. "You're a dame who can stand it when the going gets tough," she told her reflection. She wondered if this outfit was something a self-respecting lesbian would wear.

Lesbian, lesbian, lesbian, she asserted as she stared at herself. Color flared in her cheeks. Get used to it, she thought. Come on. "Hi, I'm a lesbian," she said to her reflection. The woman in the mirror looked too perky to be a lesbian. Carolyn wondered if she would look better if she got her hair frosted. She tried to picture herself as a blonde, or a redhead. Something exotic. Something that looked more like a lesbian somehow. "If you're a lesbian, prove it," she told the woman in the mirror.

The woman in the mirror blushed and kept on blushing. Carolyn wondered if lesbians blushed. Nick had blushed, but Nick wasn't – no, just because she wore men's clothes did not mean she was a lesbian. But why had Nick kissed her – oh, it was hardly a kiss. Dwelling on it was making her crazy. "Every woman you meet is not a lesbian," she told herself sternly. She had thought, throughout the day, she had seen literally hundreds of real, substantial, gorgeous women she was certain were all lesbians. She sighed, then realized the time and hurried away from her reflection and the telltale blush.

The ticket Nick had promised was waiting for her, and she was given admittance to the main building of the baroque palace. With a sigh, she walked slowly up the marble Cherub's Staircase to the main ballroom. Once there she found no sign of Nick so she fought her way to the bar and returned to the valued windows of the main ballroom hall with a glass of champagne. She sipped and wrinkled her nose as the bubbles tickled. The skyline was low, but punctuated with steeples and spires silhouetted in the last of the evening light. In the reflection of

119

the glass she gazed over the crowd and tried to pick out any woman who looked like she might also be a lesbian.

No one stood out from the crowd. One woman was particularly lovely — slight and graceful like a dancer with pale golden hair. Couldn't possibly be a lesbian, Carolyn decided, but nevertheless she could feel heat suffusing her face and she imagined slipping the spaghetti straps off the milky white shoulders. Stop that, she commanded herself. It's rude. She refocused her eyes and concentrated on the skyline for a few minutes.

At last she spotted Nick nodding politely as three older men all talked at once around her. Carolyn found it incredible that no one had guessed Nick was a woman when it was so obvious to Carolyn now. But then Nick was unusually tall for a woman, and with that height, the severe expression, long nose and very short hair, there was little to betray the truth. Her hands might have, but now that Carolyn thought about it, she'd never studied them when Nick wasn't wearing white gloves. Carolyn stared at the jacket which concealed every hint of womanly attributes. The striped tie and stiff white shirt dropped without swelling from neck to waist. The tuxedo slacks were cut fashionably baggy so neither from the front or back did Nick's figure look anything other than masculine. Carolyn successfully controlled a blush as she contemplated seeing Nick as nature had made her.

Across the room Nick suddenly looked up and caught her staring. Nick gave her a guarded smile and within a few minutes headed her way. Just as Nick stepped up to her someone called Nick's name.

Carolyn and Nick both looked toward the voice. A flashbulb went off and Nick swore.

"Bloody hell. I'm sorry, I didn't mean for that to happen. Maybe when we first met it would have been okay, but not now."

Carolyn was blinking, trying to get her eyesight back. "Who was that?"

"Some society reporter, no doubt. Let's hope something else is more interesting for tomorrow's paper."

Carolyn let Nick guide her out to the balcony, then along the curve until they were away from the open doors and brilliant lights of the party. They were partially screened by potted trees.

"Nick, what did you mean it would have been okay in the beginning?"

"What?"

"The photograph."

"Oh." Nick flushed. "Oscar likes to see my picture in the paper."

"Or you do." Suddenly, Carolyn understood. The dinner in Munich, the kiss, the ticket tonight – they *were* just blinds for the press. "You were just using me, weren't you?" Carolyn leaned away from Nick although her body told her not to.

"I was past that idea when we first went to dinner."

"I don't ..." Carolyn stiffened as Nick put her hands on her shoulders "– believe you." The stiffness became a shudder. "Oh God, don't touch me."

"Carolyn –" Nick's voice faded away.

Carolyn thought it was Nick who leaned closer, but as her arms found their way around Nick's waist she wasn't sure. She only knew that Nick's lips were on hers, tender and soft. Carolyn moaned and pulled Nick as close as possible. She cupped Nick's cheek, then her hand slipped to Nick's throat, earning an answering moan from Nick.

Why is she kissing me, Carolyn asked herself, but even as she thought it she knew the answer didn't matter. She leaned into Nick, coiling herself in Nick's arms, ready for more of this incredible sweetness. Her mouth invited Nick to explore. Nick kissed her deeper and harder. Carolyn, still thinking coherently in a very small part of her brain, wondered if Nick knew Carolyn was kissing her because she knew Nick was a woman.

She arched into the circle of Nick's arms. Nick arched in answer. Her lips answered instinctively while her brain continued to reason through the obvious: Nick knew Carolyn was a woman and that she herself was a woman. So while Nick might not know Carolyn's reasons, she knew her own. Nick *was* a lesbian. She had to be to kiss another woman like this. Carolyn shuddered at the reality of a woman's body so close and so hard against her own, hips rocking hers.

Her hand dropped further from Nick's throat, lower until it came to a thin layer she could feel through Nick's shirt. Then she slipped her fingers slightly lower until she felt what should not have been there, not if Nick was a man. She left her hand there, trembling as she thought of Nick's shirt open, the layers gone and the soft swell under her palm.

Nick groaned, rocking Carolyn in her arms. Carolyn wanted to tell Nick she knew, but it would

have meant ending that delicious, breathless kiss.
She didn't want it to end. Neither, apparently, did
Nick. It deepened and went on. And on.

7
Magic Racket

"Nick," someone said urgently.

Nick's hands were at Carolyn's back, arching her up into her arms. "Nick, stop that," the voice said again. Nick raised her head. Carolyn felt a cool breeze blow over her damp lips.

"Damn you," Nick said. Carolyn realized with a daze that Oscar was standing next to them, between them and the party. More people had come out onto the balcony since they had and some were looking their way. "You have no right, Oscar."

"If you must do this, then the least you could do is find the back seat of a car," Oscar said, his tone crushing.

Carolyn blushed furiously and turned her head. "I have to go," she said.

"No," Nick said. "Stay."

"Nick, you don't know why —" Carolyn said. "My concert . . ."

"And you don't either." Nick glared at Oscar then turned back to Carolyn. "Let's leave together then."

"No," Carolyn said. "You have to stay. I just can't bear any more flashbulbs."

"Don't go," Nick said. "Please wait, why did you kiss me?"

"Because I wanted to, that's why. Though lord knows why." Carolyn's embarrassment turned to anger. "You calculating son-of-a-bitch! You want us to be seen."

"Not *son*-of-a-bitch."

Oscar hissed. "Nicolas!"

"Oh I know that," Carolyn snapped. "But I'm not going to be your . . . your cover!"

"You know . . ." Nick said in a dazed voice. "You know, and you still kissed me like that?"

Carolyn stared at Nick and realized Nick was breathing hard and fast. "I said I kissed you because I wanted to," she said defiantly. "I guessed while we were having dinner in The Hague. It . . . was an illuminating moment."

"How?"

"When I mentioned pantyhose, you blushed."

"Nick, if you must have this conversation perhaps you should leave. People are coming this way," Oscar said under his breath.

Nick's eyes closed for a few moments then opened again, her gaze fixing on Carolyn. "Exposed by pantyhose. My God." Nick's expression softened. "Please stay, and after the concert we'll go somewhere and ... talk."

"I won't pose for pictures," Carolyn said. Her body didn't want to leave, but her pride told her that everything couldn't be Nick's way. "I have my own ticket ..."

"Whatever it is, it's second rate," Nick said with a smile more like the Nick Carolyn was used to. "Please, Carolyn ... stay with me." Oscar exhaled in a hiss of disapproval and stalked way.

The world faded to Nick's lips again. With the memory of their softness flooding her body, Carolyn said yes, she would stay.

The rest of the evening was a painful and unreal blur. She sat in Nick's box but her mind was not caught by the Rachmaninoff, not this time. She gave up trying to absorb the music and studied Nick's rigid back instead.

When the concert was over, she took her time getting backstage and waited near the door for Nick. She wouldn't meet Oscar's gaze — not that he came within ten feet of her. When Nick was finally ready to go, Carolyn virtually ran for the door. Her silk suit didn't combat much of the cool evening air, but she was sweating nevertheless.

"Shall we walk?"

"Please." Carolyn kept her head down and

plodded along. When Nick suddenly grabbed her, she jumped.

"You're crossing against the light," Nick said.

Carolyn looked at the light and then at Nick. She swayed when she studied the jacket, remembering what she had felt underneath it. She swallowed. "Why are you dressed like that?"

Nick took a deep breath and said in a rush, "The male hierarchical control of the music industry and all aspects of performing and recording, including the symphonic podium, extending to the production of music which excludes the presence of female artists and interpretations."

Carolyn found she could laugh. "You've been practicing, haven't you?"

"I figure when the news finally breaks, I'm going to have to fit into a ten-second bite on BBC-One. If I'm ever famous enough."

"I've never ..." Carolyn cleared her throat. "When I guessed that night that you were ... a woman ... I felt relieved and then I realized what that meant."

"What does it mean?" Nick caught Carolyn's gaze in a long, steady look that was by far their most intimate exchange to date. Calm settled on Carolyn and she felt in control of her body, in control of her desires. The next was a hard step, and she would not be able to say later that she'd done what was expected, that she'd bowed to the romance of the situation.

She was choosing.

"That I want you because you're a woman," she said quietly. "Since the moment I knew ... your secret, I've been very, very attracted to you. I've never felt that men were a part of my life and now I know why. But it's new to me. I've known the truth about myself for less time than I've known you — counting from the moment I almost threw up on your feet."

"I was beastly," Nick said, her voice distracted. Red blotches of emotion stained her cheeks, forehead and throat.

Carolyn smiled. "Yes, you were. You were so *macho* I hated you."

"I'm sorry." Nick shook her head. She started when a car honked in traffic. "We can't stand here all night. Can I come back to your hotel?"

The tenderness in Nick's voice set off a chain reaction of prickling in Carolyn's back and ears that would have shocked her even yesterday, but she welcomed it, encouraged the electric waves. *I'm alive ... at last.* "It's very impersonal. I doubt anyone would notice if I took a football team up to my room as long as I was quiet."

"Are you taking me up to your room?" Nick's voice was low.

"Yes," Carolyn said. "To talk." She crossed the street, sensing Nick behind her. In the dim light of the next block she put her hand on Nick's arm. She was amazed to feel Nick shudder, and was aware again of her control and her choice. "My body is telling me I'm ready for more, but my head is way behind."

"Your body could help your mind catch up."

"I don't think it works that way."

"It did for me. God bless Sister Patrick Rose, wherever she is," Nick said, with a slight laugh in her voice. "But I'll behave, if you want me to."

They slipped through the lobby of Carolyn's hotel, attracting only a nod from the doorman. In her room Carolyn turned on the lamp at the desk and the lamp next to the bed. The glare of incandescent light banished every shred of romantic ambiance.

Nick sat down in the neutral zone created by two uncomfortable chairs and a small table near the only window. Carolyn almost sat down on the bed, but thought better of it. She sat down at the table, too, and then had to smile because it appeared so businesslike.

There was a long silence. Carolyn broke it by saying, "I thought you needed to talk."

Nick stared at Carolyn's hands for a long moment, then shook her head. "I lied. I didn't want to say goodnight."

"I don't either, but I'm not ... ready." There's so much I have to sort out, she wanted to say. There's Alison and Samantha and how can I be sure it's *you* I'm drawn to, and not just your body. Carolyn realized she had no idea how Nick's body really looked. Her mind, unasked, began drawing surprisingly detailed pictures of how it *could* look, and then urged Carolyn to invite Nick to let her compare imagination with reality. She shook her head violently to clear it. "I can't, at least not tonight."

Nick flushed. "Carolyn, I want you," she said, meeting Carolyn's gaze again, and the intimacy of her eyes made Carolyn waver. "The last thing I want to do is sound like a man, but I'll have to know what you want, soon, so I can deal with it. We don't have a lot of time."

"That's only fair," Carolyn said. She clasped her hands on the table. Business-like. *You saved your virginity for thirty years and what did that get you? What's holding you back?* "I don't know."

"Don't know what?"

"I don't know why, but I feel deep down that tonight's not right. I know I want you, Nick." Carolyn blushed slightly. "But I don't know if I love you." *So, I haven't changed. I still want the romance.*

Nick laughed, and ran one hand through her hair. "As a popular song from a few years back asked, what's love got to do with it? Carolyn, I don't know if I love you. I just know this intense wanting doesn't happen too often."

"Nick," Carolyn whispered, her hands gripping the edge of the table. "Nick, you have to go." She stood up. "I promise we'll resolve this tomorrow. I know," she stammered, "that by this time tomorrow we'll ..." She waved at the bed. "But I haven't been preparing." Her voice faded away.

"How so?" Nick's brow wrinkled in amused perplexity.

"I, well, I haven't shaved my legs recently, for beginners."

"Sweetheart," Nick said softly, "do you think I care? I've never shaved mine."

"*I* care. Nick, don't laugh," Carolyn pleaded. She knew she was scarlet. The "sweetheart" made her disgustingly gooey inside. "I need to be ready. I need the place, my ... everything to be ready — the first time." She repeated intensely, "It really will be my first time."

"Carolyn, I don't think I can play the role of dream lover in a romantic setting you concoct. I'm the kind of lover I am." Nick laughed suddenly. "But I'll try, lord help me, I'll try. I just realized how rusty I am. I need a shower and ... maybe I could use a little time, too. And let someone else call the tune for once."

Carolyn walked Nick to the door of her room. "Thank you," she said, unable to meet Nick's gaze. "I can't believe I'm saying no."

"I don't really believe it myself," Nick said. "You'll come to the Cathedral tomorrow morning, won't you? Salzburg is getting the most out of me with all these extra concerts. The balcony is for spectators, and Oscar will save you room."

"What's the program?"

"Mozart's *Requiem*. Say you'll be there."

"Okay," Carolyn said. Carolyn knew she had agreed to more than Mozart. They stared at each other, then Carolyn opened the door. Nick went through it, then turned back.

"Something on account," she whispered, and her lips pressed against Carolyn's.

Carolyn gave a moan of surprise, but it wasn't surprise that made her moan when Nick stepped away and walked down the hall without a backward glance. She closed the door and touched her fingers to her lips. They felt swollen, and not as soft as Nick's had felt. She shuddered at the remembered sensation of Nick's lips, and groaned, half in want, half in irony.

She looked at the undisturbed bed and asked the

chair where Nick had been sitting, "Am I fool, or what?"

♥

Nick awoke to Oscar's quiet wake-up knock and was amazed that she had slept. She let Oscar know she was up, and as she stumbled into her bathroom, she was torn between annoyance at having to get up for the early mass and a joyful singing in her head that had nothing to do with Mozart and everything to do with Carolyn. Her body actually felt as if she'd been run over by a lorry, but early mornings could do that. She stretched and prepared herself for the concert.

The early mass was the equivalent of a dress rehearsal to Nick, though she knew the Bishop probably didn't think of it that way. During the time between the early and late masses, Nick reviewed a very abbreviated list of last-minute instructions with the choir and the chamber musicians who were arranged to the left of the choir, under the organ. She wanted to turn and search for Carolyn in the balcony, but she didn't because she wasn't sure what she'd do if Carolyn wasn't there. And she wasn't sure what she'd do if Carolyn *was* there.

You're about to perform, she told herself. Concentrate on your performance. Concentrate on the vocalists who are counting on you, and the musicians who are waiting to follow the tip of your baton wherever it leads. She breathed slowly and deeply, letting her mind be ordered by the opening parts of the service. She kept her mind focused on the music to come.

If the popularized version of Mozart's life was anything like reality, writing this requiem had killed him. It was both a rage against death and a plea for mercy and compassion. Thanks to the sisters at the orphanage, she knew the pattern of high mass backwards and forwards and the ritual was calming — the Anglican version was only slightly different from the Catholic. At the appointed time she strode to the podium, raised her baton, and summoned the attention of the organist, first violin and choirmaster.

Nick had always believed that music was power; she had believed it from the first day she had made a violin do what she wanted. The magic of the moment had ruined any chance she might have had for a more prosaic career. As the organ swelled into the massive dome of the cathedral, she felt the power of the tones surging, but it didn't stop with her body. Her baton seemed to glow, tracing a lighted path through the air. Afterglow lines showed where the baton had been, and she had never felt such an acute awareness of the concentration of the other performers on her, how their energy was directed at her, through her, and out of her again. When the music paused she could feel the music to come seething to escape.

And it escaped — she was conducting music, conducting electricity, conducting light. Her intensity, instead of collapsing inward like a black hole, exploded outward — a nova that sang through her fingertips and haloed the choir and musicians. Her entire body was caught up in the magic; she rose to her tiptoes again and again, reaching higher in an agony of ecstasy. *Recordare, Ingemisco, Confutatis.*

During the *Libera Me* the magic came unbound — it crashed in waves of light and sound through Nick, and then filled the nave, swelled through the chancel and then up into the great dome, carrying Nick's senses with it. When the baton quivered at the last note, she came back to herself. The light faded as she lowered the baton. She wondered, then, if she had imagined the glow and the power.

The cathedral was utterly silent — then the sounds of hundreds of people breathing in slowly, as if waking from deep sleep, filled Nick's ears and she realized she had not heard the music, only felt it.

She went quickly to her seat in the choir again, and could only stare at the baton she should have left on the music stand. When the service ended she stood and shook hands with the choirmaster, who looked as dazed as Nick felt, then winced at the enthusiastic handshake of the first violinist.

"Mr. Frost, my card," an older man in sober attire said, and Nick took it, glancing automatically down at it, but her eyes did not decipher the writing. "May I call on you at your hotel tomorrow?"

"Mr. Smythe handles all my appointments," Nick said automatically. Suddenly Oscar was there, face aglow with some strong emotion. "Oscar, this gentleman would like an appointment tomorrow." She handed him the card.

Oscar's eyes widened when he read the card. Then, after an intense look of fierce pride Nick could only marvel at, walked a few steps away to discuss times with the owner of the card. She greeted other people, and evidently said the right things though she couldn't have remembered a face or a word.

Finally, after what seemed like an endless stream of people, one particular pair of blue eyes shone at her and Nick saw the trace of tears on Carolyn's face. She moved closer to Carolyn.

"What is it?" She traced a line of the tears with her thumb.

Carolyn, moving it seemed to Nick in slow motion, put her hand on Nick's cheek. "Yes, you're real," she said. "Nick ... it was magic. Magic," she repeated. "I can't find the words."

"You felt it, too," Nick asked softly.

"*Everyone* felt it. I think I didn't breathe."

"I feel as if I didn't." Nick took a deep breath and felt the haze around her dissolve. "I need air." She put her arm around Carolyn; it felt the most natural thing in the world to do, and they walked up the main aisle side by side.

Carolyn stayed in the circle of Nick's arm, blinking at the bright, crystal sunshine that sparkled around them. They walked slowly to the fountain in the middle of the cathedral square and stood for a moment.

"I felt like the instrument of greater power," Nick said quietly, with a kind of startled reverence. "*Her* power, from the earth to the sky." She shook her head. "The nuns are spinning in their graves. I was a theological failure."

"If that's what it takes to make music like that ... Nick, I've never heard or felt anything like it."

Nick squeezed Carolyn for a moment. "I was

blessed by a school matron who loved good music and encouraged music-making in all the girls. If I'd had a family they might not have been so patient with a caterwauling violin." She shook her head again, trying to clear it. "I don't know why I'm babbling about that. It's just that this morning may be the first time that I've understood that everything is for a reason. I experienced the very first taste of why, maybe, I exist. I suppose that sounds foolish."

"No. I think you're lucky. And everyone who hears you along the way is also very lucky."

Nick turned Carolyn to her, then after a moment's hesitation during which Carolyn could have stepped away, she kissed her.

Carolyn's mouth trembled under hers, then the soft lips tightened with intent, capturing Nick's mouth in return, opening and inviting. The kiss became sweeter still as Nick tasted Carolyn's mouth, then surrendered to the gentle brush of Carolyn tasting her, slowly, thoroughly.

Carolyn's hands slid under Nick's jacket and touched her where she hadn't been touched in years. Aware suddenly of the layers of gauze obscuring her breasts, and the T-shirt that further blunted the contours of her body, Nick broke away, gasping.

"Nick," Carolyn murmured, "I want to very much, but I don't think I can undress you right here in the square."

"I agree." Nick tried to sound carefree, but she failed miserably. "Come back to the hotel and I'll clean up and then we'll go out somewhere for lunch."

"I know what I want for lunch," Carolyn said with a laugh, "and they don't serve it in any restaurant I've ever been to."

Nick stared at Carolyn. Her smile was pure invitation. Where had this self-assured, flirtatious woman come from? "You take my breath away," Nick said.

Carolyn flashed a happy grin at Oscar as they rejoined him in the cathedral. Oscar had been disapproving and aloof when Carolyn had arrived, but then the music had washed over them both until Oscar had taken and held her hand tightly until the last note. Oscar returned her smile then looked at Nick.

"You don't know who that gentleman was, do you?"

"I glanced at the card, but I doubt I could have read anything at that moment."

"Deutsche Grammophon," Oscar said. He said it as if he were announcing Her Majesty the Queen.

Nick went very still, and Carolyn looked from Nick to Oscar. "What does that mean?"

"A recording contract," Nick whispered. "Maybe."

"I'd say definitely," Oscar said. "Nick, you gave the finest performance of that work I've ever heard."

"You've never said that before," Nick whispered.

"One expression, one sound out of many," Oscar said, as if searching for words.

"I had no idea. I didn't hear a note." Nick groped to a seat and went so pale that Carolyn was alarmed.

She dropped to Nick's side, taking her hand. "Nick, what's wrong?"

"Nothing." She cupped Carolyn's face with a

trembling hand. "I just can't believe this is happening. After so much waiting. Just a little longer and I could be ... free."

Oscar said, "I suggest that privacy would be welcome for all of us."

"Yes," Carolyn said. "It's time to have ... lunch." She pulled Nick to her feet and shivered at the electricity that still seemed to emanate from Nick's body. "I can hardly wait."

8

Rhapsodié en Bleu

Nick felt lightheaded and weak when they finally reached the suite, and no matter what Carolyn wanted, food was a priority. She excused herself for a shower and went into the bathroom, stripping away her shirt, her T-shirt, then the wrapping of gauze that smoothed her form into a nearly flat plain. As always, Nick was grateful when her breasts unflattened. She must have been distracted to have wrapped them so tightly — they were sore.

She plunged her hands under the tap, hoping the shock of the cold water would make her feel more earthly. She rubbed her face with her hands then unzipped her trousers, and pushed the rest of the clothes to the floor. As she kicked the boxer shorts away her gaze caught — and she stared down at the bloodstain for a full minute before the significance hit her. She clutched the edge of the sink.

It's not fair. It can't be that time!

But it was. She realized she'd been having all the symptoms but hadn't recognized them. Her body was about to embark on its ritual nausea, cramps and weakness. Even as she gave thanks for her body having waited through this morning, Nick felt the first tightening and ache. Her passion-flower libido wilted. *Oh bother.* There was no way she'd be making love with Carolyn for at least three days.

Nick fumbled in her pseudo-shaving kit for ibuprofen and downed several tablets. Now she needed food, and fast. Wrapped in a towel, she stepped to the door of the bathroom and called out to Carolyn.

"Nick," Carolyn said, her eyes round. "This is a surprise."

"I don't have good news," Nick said.

"You don't look good," Carolyn said more seriously.

"I feel lousy. The performance either held it off or brought it on, I don't know which, but ..." Nick grinned sheepishly when Carolyn laughed.

"Oh my God — for a conductor, you have a poor sense of timing."

Nick was relieved at Carolyn's laughter. "The ultimate proof of my womanhood. Maybe the pure woman-power helped this morning, but right now I'm about to become a miserable bear. I need food, and fast, or I might throw up on *your* shoes."

"Oscar and I will fix you up — go shower, then put on something comfy and warm."

Nick heard their muffled conversation as she toweled off a few minutes later, and pulled on her only androgynous attire — velour sweatpants and matching sweatshirt in dark gray. She left herself unbound, as it were, and despite the growing discomfort of the cramps, she still felt a flush of desire as Carolyn stared at her with frank admiration. Maybe they could go in for some passionate petting ... but even as the hope flickered Nick shuddered and groped for the softest nearby chair while her uterus tried to turn inside out. The wave passed and left her covered in a cold sweat and praying that her empty stomach would process the pills all that much faster.

"Here's some water, and room service is bringing fresh bread and *pottage du poulet.*" At Nick's frown, Carolyn smiled and said, "Chicken soup."

Nick lifted her head, then gratefully burrowed it into the pillow Carolyn plumped behind her. Some superwoman, she told herself as she succumbed to more mothering in one afternoon than she'd had in years and years. She could get used to it.

"I don't want to go, you know, but you need a good night's sleep. I'd just keep you awake," Carolyn told Nick, but she didn't try to hide the flush that swept over her when she considered the many ways she would keep Nick awake — none of which were fair to Nick. "You look as if you want to die, and you have the very important date with a recording executive tomorrow, remember? Not to mention another performance tomorrow night."

Oscar had retired for the evening some time ago, and Carolyn slowly stroked Nick's hair as Nick cuddled under a blanket up against Carolyn's thigh. "Don't leave. You keep me warm."

"I need a good night's sleep, too. While you rehearse I'm going to finish sightseeing — I have two museums to see and Oscar and I are going to finish the Mozart tour we started while you were napping.

"Sounds lovely," Nick said sleepily.

How could anyone not know Nick was a woman? Her hair was silk, and the pale fuzz on her neck was equally soft against Carolyn's fingertips. She thought she could have sat there all night, just touching, tenderly, learning the brush of Nick's hair against her fingertips. But she caught her head drooping and she nudged Nick gently. "Come on you, let's put you to bed."

"Umm. Sounds heavenly." Nick slowly got to her feet. "I don't usually pamper myself like this. It feels damn good."

Carolyn followed Nick into her bedroom, then sat on the bed until Nick emerged from the bathroom. Carolyn took the glass after Nick swallowed more tablets, then asked, "What do you sleep in?"

Nick laughed drowsily and indicated a worn T-shirt. Carolyn handed it over, and didn't look away as Nick changed. Her imagination had been very accurate.

"I could get used to this," Nick said as Carolyn tucked her in and kissed her forehead. "But I want a proper kiss."

"I'm not sure I know how to kiss properly," Carolyn said, her lips trying to turn her uncertainty into a joke, but Nick didn't smile back.

"You know how," Nick said.

Carolyn breathed in slowly and leaned down. She covered Nick's mouth with her own, light and lingering.

"Very nice," Nick breathed.

"Quick study," Carolyn said. "Good night."

She let herself out into the quiet hotel, then walked the well-lit street to her own hotel. Nick filled her mind when she closed her eyes to sleep, and the scent of Nick's body, warm and damp after her shower, surrounded her. She breathed it in, enjoying the intoxication. *If this isn't love, I like it anyway.*

♥

"Devon, I'm ready! Shake a leg!" Alison checked her satchel one last time for her passport and tickets. Devon locked the office door and hopped down the stairs.

"There's ninety minutes before your flight, and it's a twenty-minute drive," Devon said reprovingly. "The last few days you've been about as much fun as income taxes."

"Sorry," Alison said shortly. "This trip means a lot to me." She hadn't told Devon much, but she knew she'd been more moody than usual.

"Don't think I don't know why," Devon said. He

hoisted one of the suitcases into the voluminous trunk of his Dodge Dart. "You're being oh-so-secretive about this trip, but I know what you're up to. 'Why don't you take a week off, Devon? Wouldn't a vacation be nice, Devon?'" he mimicked. "You're going to romp in Europe while I swelter in this gawdawful heat wave."

"Could you just get in the car," Alison pleaded.

Devon glared at her, but got in. "I haven't asked, but what will it mean if Miss Love-Among-the-Roses actually decides you are worth sleeping with?"

"I don't know what you mean," Alison said, pretending not to recognize the title of Carolyn's first book.

"Have it your way, but you're going out on a long, long limb and while she's very nice, and has always been friendly, she still never struck me as liking queer trees. I hope you know what you're doing."

Alison drew in a shuddering breath and said nothing. At the airport she gave the sulky Devon a hug. "I've been a bitch to live with. But wish me luck."

"Okay, I'll wish you luck, and some oral sex. And thanks for my week off."

Alison laughed and hugged Devon again. "Hope you have some oral sex too."

The long journey gave Alison time to think, especially since reading the work she'd brought with her was as unappealing as the airline food.

The airport in Frankfort, where she changed

flights, was shockingly like any other. Here, however, the signs were in a half-dozen languages — in the States they sometimes deigned to add another language, but one non-English language seemed to be the limit. Her layover was four hours, so she went in search of food and formulated Alison's First Theorem of Traveling, which stated in its entirety: Stale tortilla chips encrusted with pasteurized, processed, artificially flavored cheese product by any other name still tastes like shit. *Der nachos.* They were salty and artificial and therefore tasted a lot like her usual dinners, which as a rule came from boxes, bags or buckets.

She realized her preoccupation with the food kept her from wondering if she was making the all-time big mistake. She ignored her subconscious, which kept telling her she was making a fool of herself. When it wouldn't cooperate she tried reasoning with it. Perceive this, she said sternly. If this trip turns out to be the most colossal waste of money I've ever achieved, you may say I told you so and I'll listen to what you've been saying about getting a life. But give me until Rome.

Her subconscious continued to mutter doubts.

♥

"Because I promised myself I would stick to my itinerary," Carolyn said stubbornly.

Nick was flabbergasted. "But you didn't know you'd — we'd —"

"No, but I keep promises, even to myself. I told you why."

Nick didn't see what Carolyn's ill-fated marriage

had to do with her. "But I'm not what's-his-name. I'm —"

"A woman pretending to be a man. And I'm a l-lesbian." Carolyn's frown softened into a smile. "I obviously need to practice that."

Nick was relieved to see the smile. "I know we're a very odd couple, but darling, I don't see why we can't travel together. Why can't you just check into my suite when we get to Rome? If you take the flight you're booked on, I'll be away from you for almost a day before we connect again."

"I know. I regret the waste of a day, too. But Nick — it just seems so much like before. Wait, let me finish. I know that inside I'm totally changed. I know that when we finally — you know —"

"After the performance tonight, if you'll just stay —"

"I know it'll be right. Just as everything with my marriage was wrong. But the situation, the holiday romance thing — it feels just the same. I distrust it."

Nick didn't know what to do or what to say. She didn't want to lose one precious moment with Carolyn — not when Carolyn's holiday was coming to a close after Rome, and Nick was, if Deutsche Grammophon followed up on the tantalizing expressions of interest, shortly going to be committed to a recording session. "I understand. But what can I say? I don't want you to go. And when we get to Rome, I don't want you in another hotel — I want you in my bed."

"You'll be welcome in my bed, you know." Carolyn turned her head slightly, and Nick couldn't see her expression.

146

"But darling, it makes more sense if you stay with me."

"Why?" Her face was still hidden.

"Because, it'll seem more ... natural, I guess." Nick said it reluctantly, hoping Carolyn would understand.

"Oh God." Carolyn stood up and walked to the windows of Nick's bedroom. "I keep forgetting you're a man." Her laugh had no humor in it.

"I'm not ... it's just the clothes," Nick said desperately. She wanted to leap up out of her chair and run to Carolyn, hug her, but Carolyn had gone all pointy. Oh bother.

"And wanting to appear as if you have a woman staying with you. So you look just like any other normal red-blooded guy. Oh God. I'd forgotten all about that."

"Carolyn, that's not it." But it was ... partially. "It's true that I wouldn't mind our affair becoming known because it might keep anyone from more intensely scrutinizing me. But I won't sacrifice you to do that. I wouldn't ask that of you."

"And I have to fight my own well-schooled instincts to do the womanly thing and sacrifice for you and the relationship." She turned back from the window and said intensely, "Nick, don't you see, I've just discovered a brand new me, and I haven't sorted that out yet. I don't know what my new features are, what I want, jeez, what I'm going to do for a living. It's so damn tempting to run away with you and play house. It'll look so damn *normal*. It would be so easy ... but I'd never get the chance to be what I finally know I am. I can't lie."

"You'd be surprised how little I've lied."

Carolyn's eyebrows raised skeptically.

"All I have to do is wear men's clothes and say my name is Nicolas. I never call myself Mister, and I've only lied on my passport application."

"But it all equals deception. Oh Nick, it's beside the point. I know it would be easy ..."

"So why are you making it so hard on yourself?"

"So why do you wear men's clothes?" Carolyn's chin was positively mulish.

"Okay," Nick said, not understanding but recognizing that Carolyn felt strongly about it and would not change her mind. "You're leaving for Rome in a few hours. I guess I'll see you when I get there." She tried to sound light.

Carolyn walked toward Nick, her body outlined by the vivid Salzburg sky. Blue eyes gleamed at Nick. "Why don't we make the best use of the few hours before I leave?" She stopped in front of Nick, looking down at her.

Nick caught her breath when Carolyn's hands cupped her face. She bent over Nick, hair whispering off her back and draping across Nick's shoulders.

More kisses. The kisses of the last few days had been divinely excruciating. Nick had suggested, repeatedly, that while her own body was out of commission, so to speak, there was no reason why Carolyn should place similar restrictions on herself. But Carolyn had it in her head that nothing should hinder either of them.

The kisses promised that the first time would be memorable. Already Carolyn's lips nibbled at Nick's shoulders. Nick was ready for their first time. Her skin seemed to inhale Carolyn's touch. Carolyn knelt, her mouth coming hungrily to Nick's breasts —

completely unflattened and less flat with every moment — and her fingers went to Nick's shirt buttons, then her hands possessed Nick's shoulders.

"Why not now?" Carolyn's voice swirled in Nick's ear in a symphony of suggestion and desire.

"I — I want the first time to be right," Nick said. "Your romantic ideas have won me over."

"All right," Carolyn murmured. "Then just kiss me." Her lips were soft and open against Nick's mouth as she pulled Nick out of the chair. "Kiss me." She drew Nick down on top of her, hips arching up, mouth inviting . . . body so soft . . .

When Nick heard the quiet knocking she realized that it had been going on for some time. "Damn," she muttered. She rolled away from Carolyn and rebuttoned her shirt. Carolyn, after a dazed, frozen moment, got unsteadily to her feet, and went back to the window.

Nick smoothed her hair as she went to the door, knowing Oscar would not have knocked if it weren't important. Of course Oscar wouldn't know what he'd interrupted, but then again Oscar was no fool either. She opened the door, listened, then bolted to the bathroom. In less than sixty seconds, Maestro Frost emerged.

Carolyn still stood at the window, her expression lost in the shadow. She didn't say anything as Nick smiled at her and mouthed, "Deutsche Grammophon again," but she did show Nick that her fingers crossed for good luck. Nick took a deep breath, then entered the sitting room with a brisk air.

Nick had trouble following what the representative was saying. The memory of Carolyn's body at the window, outlined in sunlight, was foremost in her mind. She realized suddenly what she was absentmindedly agreeing to. "Two weeks from now? That's absurd!"

Deutsche Grammophon explained their situation again — the London Symphony Orchestra was already scheduled. The Royal Academy Choir was already scheduled. The scheduled legendary conductor, however, was suddenly and regrettably inflicted with gallstones and the company had found only one available conductor it felt could finish the recording session, which required symphonic competence, and, more importantly, superb choral control. After the concert in the Great Cathedral, well, how could Maestro Frost not agree? Maestro Frost was the only conductor available who could successfully conduct Mahler's *Symphony of a Thousand.* And Maestro Frost would share an album with the aforementioned legend.

Nick knew flattery when she heard it, but it sounded wonderful all the same. Still, two weeks — she'd have barely enough time to feel settled again in what passed for home in London. Absolutely not, she couldn't do it.

Deutsche Grammophon became very persuasive with numbers and alluded to residuals. Oscar asked him to clarify, and when he did, Nick understood that a great deal of money must already be involved. But money wasn't quite everything — her priorities *were* intact — and even as she opened her mouth to refuse one more time, Nick saw the future. She'd read a science fiction story once where the people had the ability to see all possible futures from the point in time where they stood. From where she stood, she saw only two possible futures. The future in which she refused this offer did not contain another chance.

"I'll do it — provided you can have a contract that satisfies Mr. Smythe ready by the end of the day." She was not going to Rome without knowing where she would be bound afterward.

Deutsche Grammophon promised to meet the deadline and departed. Nick stood behind the closed door and stared at Oscar, who stared back.

They gave a simultaneous whoop of joy and Oscar hugged Nick tightly. "This is it!" he exulted.

"What's up?" Carolyn stood in the bedroom doorway.

Nick whirled, then literally danced over to her. "I'm going to make a record for a very prestigious recording company. In London. With the world-famous symphony and choir located there. Tah-duh!"

Carolyn threw her arms around Nick, and Nick gathered her up, then swung her around in a circle before letting go. "It's only two weeks away."

"Two weeks!"

"They're desperate and they want me!" Nick managed a time step before she ran out of breath. "Come out to dinner and celebrate."

"Nick," Carolyn said slowly, "I'm leaving for Rome. In fact, I really should be getting back to my hotel."

"No!" Nick's enthusiasm faded as quickly as it had bloomed.

"Yes." Carolyn nodded with emphasis.

"But this is a once-in-a-lifetime celebration, Carolyn, please."

"Nick, you're one of those people whose entire life

will be one once-in-a-lifetime experience after another. I'm just ordinary Carolyn Vincense, and the life I have is the only one I've got. I've got to stick with it, for a while longer." Carolyn caught her lower lip between her teeth. "Nick, I'm sorry. It's how I feel."

"I *don't* understand."

Carolyn's expression went stormy, catching Nick offguard. "I understand how *you* feel, which makes it even harder for me to go. The least you could do is *try* to understand what I'm talking about."

"I am trying, but I just don't get it," Nick said brusquely, Carolyn's anger sparking within Nick. Only minutes ago they had been so passionate, but with completely different intent.

"Children," Oscar said reprovingly. "Arguing is pointless." Oscar put his hand on Nick's arm. "You of all people should know you can't play the composition faster than it's scored for."

"I'm the one composing it," Nick muttered.

"I'm at *least* coauthor," Carolyn said, then her mouth closed in a hard, stubborn line.

"Precisely," Oscar said. He bowed slightly to her. "I look forward to seeing you in Rome. And now I will excuse myself tactfully, hoping that you will both be sensible."

Nick waited until Oscar had left them alone, then she said, "Well, if you want to go, I suppose you should." She knew she was ungracious.

Carolyn sighed. "I don't want to, I have to. There's a difference."

"The result's the same." Nick pouted, something she hadn't done in ages.

"No, it isn't. An afternoon and evening of your

life is affected, but the shape and aspect of my entire future will be formed. We haven't talked about after Rome, and now you have this record to do and I have a life to get back to. I don't know what we'll do. I just know about today and tomorrow."

"I'll see you tomorrow afternoon, won't I?" Nick was ashamed of her unsuccessful attempt at emotional blackmail. Only two nights ago she had been seriously wondering if she should continue her masquerade — and now it seemed the masquerade might have been worth it. How could she presume Carolyn into something when she had no idea if she could let Carolyn completely into her life?

"Of course," Carolyn said. "Since you've been before, I want you to show me the Piazza at St. Peter's, and the Basilica too."

Nick laughed. "Do you have any idea how big they are?"

"No, but you'll think of something. You can be the macho man for the afternoon." Carolyn smiled easily, and Nick was glad to see the robin's-egg blue fill with teasing light.

"If I did what a macho man would do, you wouldn't see a single sight."

"You're all talk," Carolyn said, then she grabbed Nick and kissed her fiercely. "I gotta do all the action myself."

A few minutes later, as she opened the door for Carolyn, Nick said, "I suppose that absence makes the heart grow fonder."

"It does in all the romances I've ever read," Carolyn said, giving Nick one last quick kiss. "Of course, in all of those the man was considerably more macho than you are, and had a p—"

Nick said, "If you *ever* finish that sentence, I'll —"

"*Arrivederci, carrissima.*" Carolyn's laugh lingered in the hallway long after the elevator had come and gone.

♥

Nick rushed rehearsals and could only laugh to herself when she overheard two musicians agreeing that Nick was not the pain-in-the-ass they'd expected. She had trouble finding a cab, then impatiently got out a block early, certain she could move faster on foot through the congested — and vocal — Roman traffic.

She was there. Nick stopped hurrying and slowed to catch her breath. Carolyn was shading her eyes with her hand, studying the crowds and the pigeons and looking absolutely gorgeous. When she saw Nick, Carolyn waved and then came into Nick's arms, kissing and laughing about the heat and the time, and under it all Nick could sense how glad Carolyn was to see her. The feeling was mutual.

Since it was so late in the afternoon, they were only able to see a portion of St. Peter's Basilica before it closed to tourists. Nick was disappointed, since she'd really been wanting to show Carolyn the sunset from inside the dome. It was very romantic. But late afternoon clouds had rolled in and then lowered, dulling the sunset and increasing the heat. Pigeons scattered as they strolled across the Piazza. Nick was glad they could now have an early dinner. Early to bed, early to ... other things. But she had decided she was going to be British about this. She would wait for Carolyn and keep a stiff upper lip. Right-o.

"It's cooler in the shade." Nick wished she could walk around without a jacket. The humidity was unbearable. "Isn't it hot, suddenly?"

"It's getting downright uncomfortable," Carolyn said, fanning herself. "I think it's warmer now than it was an hour ago."

"It doesn't bother me," Nick said. Big lie.

"I think I'd like to come back tomorrow morning. Are you hungry?" Carolyn wiped her brow with the back of her hand.

Nick felt awash in Carolyn's blue eyes. "I'm very hungry." No lie.

"I know just the place for dinner. I asked the clerk at the gift shop in the hotel and she told me about the little cafe right around the corner. It's inexpensive but wonderful, she said. I've discovered on this trip that women know all the best places."

"Lead on, then," Nick said. She was aware of Carolyn's every breath and every movement. As they walked back toward the hotel district, the humidity increased and Nick could see a damp line down the spine of Carolyn's cotton shirt. The heat suddenly intensified and without warning, the clouds opened.

"It's tropical," Carolyn gasped. Nick started to pull her under a nearby awning, but Carolyn danced away. "No, I love the rain." She spun, letting the rain fall on her face, on her outstretched arms. Her shirt was soaked in a matter of moments.

Nick's aching want of Carolyn flared and singed her body. She caught herself against the wall, and put her arm across her stomach. She didn't know if she could walk. She wanted to capture Carolyn's hand and guide it to her body, tell her to use her fingers, beg her to drink the proof of Nick's passion.

Carolyn's hair was wet with rain as she stood in profile to Nick, face upturned, licking the rain from her lips. Nick could only breathe harder as Carolyn's bra, outlined under her soaked shirt, melted into translucency as well. When Carolyn turned to face her after a few minutes, the pale mystery of her breasts was graced by blurred points of rose. Nick wanted to fall to her knees and worship, and stay on her knees to worship lower.

"Isn't it beautiful?" Carolyn twirled once more in the rain. "And so warm. It's just like what I've always imagined Tahiti was like. Come join me." She stood still again, letting the rain run through her hair.

"I can't," Nick said. At least she tried to say it, but all her own ears heard was a groan. She stepped into the rain. The heat from the sidewalk and the heat from Carolyn's body radiated through her clothes. A fever melted her rationality and she reached for Carolyn.

Carolyn stiffened and stared at Nick. Nick's hands slid from Carolyn's shoulders to her ribs, the heels of her palms just grazing the swelling wonder of Carolyn's breasts. Carolyn's body was hot and wet, as hot and wet as Nick knew she herself was underneath the boxer shorts.

"Carolyn, I ..." Nick's fingers smoothed slowly over Carolyn's back, then ran the length of her spine. Nick pulled Carolyn closer and wiped raindrops from Carolyn's forehead. They moved together as if they were slow dancing. Nick wanted to dip Carolyn ... dip her deeply.

Almost as if she were watching and not actually doing it herself, Nick saw her fingers trace the outline of Carolyn's lips, then the smooth ridge of flesh that led from upper lip to nose. They fanned slowly across the wet cheek, up under the lashes, then down, whispering across the strong jaw line, caressing the graceful neck, gripping the firm shoulder, then pressing against the flat of Carolyn's breastbone.

Nick couldn't breathe as she contemplated the softness her hand wanted to enclose and smooth. She looked back up into Carolyn's eyes and saw wide-eyed panic there.

"Don't look like that," Nick whispered.

"I'm afraid," Carolyn said in a quavering voice. "I'm afraid we're about to get arrested."

Nick managed a nonchalant, but confidently masculine smile at the policeman who had stopped to glare at them. She muttered something appropriate about Rome and romance, then said, also in Italian, that she and the little missus would be going back to their hotel now. The policeman grunted and walked off.

Carolyn was laughing as Nick pulled her along. "You called me a tiny wife."

"I'll never get Italian. I can read it, I just can't speak it very well. I have learned, however, most of the key obscenities."

"I'll give you lessons, if you're good to me."

Nick let that pass until they were alone in the elevator in Carolyn's small hotel. It chugged its way slowly from floor to floor.

Nick trapped Carolyn in one corner, planting her hands on either side of Carolyn and murmuring in her ear. "This is how I plan to be good to you. I want to kiss you. I want to press my lips to yours and feel the soft wetness of you against my lips." She felt Carolyn tremble slightly. "I want to touch your face. I want to learn each expression and know when I am pleasing you, when you want more, when you want less." Nick moaned when Carolyn nibbled Nick's lower lip. She swayed and felt Carolyn steady her. "I want to learn your entire body with my mouth, first your lips, then your shoulders, your stomach, your breasts, then below. I want to taste you. Swim in you, love you with my mouth until you stop me or beg me to begin again."

Nick's throat constricted and she couldn't speak. Through the fog of her mind she was aware that Carolyn's hips were against her own, rocking and pressing. She looked back to Carolyn's face. The elevator seemed to be filled with steam.

The door opened and Nick released Carolyn.

"I suppose that'll do for a start," Carolyn said weakly.

Do I turn the light on, or do I leave it off? Carolyn stood just inside the door, butterflies beating hard against her heart. *Should I undress or does she undress me?* Carolyn had been dreaming of this moment, but she hadn't given a thought to important questions, such as, did she lead the way to the bedroom, or did she wait for Nick to take charge?

Nick was taking off her soaked jacket. In the dim

light, Carolyn could see Nick's fingers unbuttoning her shirt and pulling it out of her pants.

"Nick," she said, her voice a faint quiver. Nick's fingers paused at the zipper of her pants. "I don't know what to do." Carolyn thought she might cry — fear, anxiety and a fierce passionate hope joined forces to ruin what little she had left of her composure.

"Darling," Nick said softly. She came to where Carolyn stood by the door. She gave Carolyn a kiss meant as reassuring, but it only increased Carolyn's awkwardness. "You've been so outrageous these last few days I forgot. I don't want to rush you."

"It's just ... I don't know what to do," Carolyn said, her voice trailing away. She gazed past Nick at the orange and terra cotta glow the sun had left in the sky over the city as it crept just under the cloud cover.

Nick said, "Let's take it slow."

Nick drew her toward the bedroom, but Carolyn hesitated. She reached down deep inside herself for courage and hoped Nick wouldn't laugh. "No, wait." Nick arched one eyebrow indulgently. Carolyn discovered she could smile. "Come and kiss me in front of the sunset."

They moved quietly together. The loudest sound was a soft gasp from Nick as Carolyn pressed her wet shirt against Nick's breast. Carolyn stood on her tiptoes, pulled Nick's head down, her mouth slightly open, inviting.

Nick gently bit Carolyn's lower lip, then pulled Carolyn hard against her. Carolyn returned the gentle bite, then hungrily tasted Nick's mouth, relieved at the reemergence of the fierce desire she felt for Nick. Her stage fright disappeared.

Carolyn kissed Nick until she couldn't breathe, her hands cupping Nick's face, fingers smoothing the hair still damp from the rain. Each kiss was a newly lit match, flaring with heat. Carolyn felt Nick's hands on her back, then Nick's fingers sliding under her waistband. The sky darkened to purple as Carolyn pulled Nick to the floor, rolling on top of Nick for one more deep and trembling kiss.

Nerves Carolyn had never known she had were prickling with sensation. Her hand went to the crotch of Nick's pants, pressing in. She was flushed with the power she suddenly felt, encouraged by Nick's groan and the response of her hips.

"I didn't know," Carolyn murmured. She straddled Nick and hurriedly pulled off her wet blouse and bra.

"You're beautiful," Nick gasped. "Stop ... too fast."

"No," Carolyn said. She knelt over Nick and her hand went back to the crotch of Nick's pants. She drew in a deep, hissing breath when Nick's hands found her bare breasts. Nick's fingers teased and pleasured.

Carolyn had nothing but instinct, but she knew that Nick's shuddering gasps meant Carolyn was doing something right. She didn't want to stop, but her fingers wanted more than cloth. Clumsily, she pulled at the button and zipper of Nick's pants, then reached in. She was momentarily taken aback at the unexpected roominess of Nick's boxer shorts, but her hand took advantage of the situation, sliding downward. Then her fingers found the fevered, wet flesh between Nick's legs.

"Car ... oh! Don't stop," Nick said from between clenched teeth. "There ..." Her voice came from deep in the back of her throat.

Carolyn rejoiced in the slippery wetness. Her body was racked with a fierce and singing joy. "I didn't know," she said again. "I didn't know." So soft, so vulnerable. Nick's body froze, then surged up. Gentle, Carolyn thought, but frighteningly strong.

Nick fell back to the floor, groaning. "I'm sorry, I'm sorry," she said.

"Why? What's wrong?"

"I was supposed to show you ... I was supposed to ..."

Carolyn laughed gently. "Looks like I got to the baton first, maestro." She slowly withdrew her fingers, laughter fading as Nick shuddered. Her fingers were covered with Nick's wetness. Carolyn stared at them in wonder, then the smell of sex overwhelmed her and she raised her hand to her lips, tasting and smelling. Her head whirled from intoxication.

She studied Nick's body, naked at last. Long, lean legs gave way to hollowed hip bones. Nick pulled Carolyn's hand down to one breast. Carolyn gasped at the erotic contrast of Nick's melting, soft breast and hard, aroused nipple.

She moved over Nick, her mouth caressing at last the swells that Nick hid away from the world. Her mouth was alive with sensation, her tongue reveling over the texture of Nick's skin. She trailed the tip of her tongue across smooth stomach, then bit gently into the tantalizing softness of Nick's hips. *This* was pleasure of the flesh. This languid and frantic mixture of tasting and teasing was the magic she'd written about and now experienced for herself for the first time.

"Carolyn, let's at least get on the bed," Nick gasped. She pulled Carolyn up into her arms again and kissed her. Carolyn moaned, kissing back, then her tongue was tracing Nick's mouth as her hand slipped again into the center of Nick's wetness.

Carolyn shuddered. Her fingers swam in Nick's pleasure. She brought her wet fingers to her lips again, smelling the sweetness, tasting. She gasped and savored, then painted Nick's breast with the wetness.

Nick groaned and said, "You're killing me, driving me crazy."

"I had no idea," Carolyn said in a daze. Her mouth was dry and she swallowed convulsively. She felt a driving thirst then, for more of Nick. Her heartbeat nearly choked her as she moved down Nick's body. She had never felt this focused on anything in her life. Tasting Nick ... she had to taste Nick now.

Satiny liquid slid over her tongue, then filled her mouth. Her lips glided over silken ripples. Nick's hips arched up and Carolyn held onto them, her tongue seeking upward. She knew she had found the right place when Nick cried out. Nick's hands were in her hair, then holding her head as Carolyn clung to Nick's shaking thighs.

She kept her arms around Nick's hips long after they had stopped moving. She had never believed she could give another person so much pleasure and derive so much pleasure for herself. Her mouth felt raw, every nerve alive. Her own hips moved at the thought of taking Nick's wetness in her mouth again, tasting the sweet-salt passion again.

"First time, my eye," Nick said in a dreamy voice. "You've done this before and don't lie. You're a bleedin' expert."

"I'm not kidding, Nick," Carolyn said. Regretfully, she sat up. "I just . . . well, maybe I'm a natural." She hoped her smile was sultry.

"I'd swear to it," Nick said. Suddenly she was on her feet and pulling Carolyn up beside her.

"What are you doing?" Carolyn murmured the question through a lazy kiss on Nick's shoulder.

"Taking you to bed."

Sheets had never felt so sensual to Carolyn's back, but they were nothing compared to the feeling of Nick's body on hers. She melted into the bed and stretched. Nick's lips brushed her chin, her eyelids, her nose. Carolyn could feel her heartbeat in her fingertips as she grasped Nick's arms.

Nick's arms slid under her waist and Carolyn gave herself up to vertigo as they rolled over. Her thighs held Nick between them. She groaned. Then she was falling again.

She landed safely in the cradle of Nick's arms. She looked up into Nick's face and resisted the temptation to close her eyes as Nick's hand slowly slid down her side, over her hips. Their gaze was locked. Carolyn saw the flare in Nick's eyes as Nick's fingers touched her. She remembered to breathe and gasp air. When Nick's fingers slid deeper, she saw the tremor of Nick's lower lip, a match to her own. Deeper still, then stroking pleasure. Carolyn wanted to kiss Nick, but if she did she wouldn't be able to gaze into her face and see every new sensation Nick gave her reflected there. At the very last moment Carolyn raised her mouth to Nick's, tasting the groaning answer as Carolyn surged against Nick's body.

She closed her eyes then and floated for a few minutes. Even breathing was sublime ecstasy. She smiled. So this was what all the fuss was about.

"What are you thinking?" Nick's voice was soft.

"That what you just did was perfect."

"I'm not finished," Nick said huskily.

Carolyn opened her eyes to catch Nick staring hungrily at her breasts. She drew Nick's head down with a groaning, "Please." At the touch of Nick's tongue she shuddered at the shock of sweetness, so good.

Every stroke of Nick's tongue increased the wetness between Carolyn's legs as she imagined that tongue, those same strokes touching her there. "Nick, oh please," she moaned. When Nick raised her head Carolyn stared at the slightly parted lips. She felt the rise and fall of Nick's chest against her and Nick gasped for breath.

Carolyn sank into the bedclothes as Nick's hair, soft from rainwater, brushed the insides of her thighs. Her body was limp except for her hips, straining toward Nick. Then her legs came alive, twining around Nick's body, drawing her down. Her arms found the strength to move and she ran her fingers through Nick's hair, then her hands held

Nick tighter to her body as Nick's tongue discovered every secret place and hidden nerve.

"Was it ... okay that I stared at you," Carolyn asked, her cheek resting on Nick's chest. "While you were ... when you first touched me."

She felt a ripple pass through Nick's body and looked up shyly as Nick answered. "That was probably the most erotic thing I've ever shared with anyone," Nick said in a soft tone of wonder. "I could see what I was doing reflected in your face."

Carolyn's head reeled as she pulled herself across Nick's body. "Then look at me," she said, her voice taut with desire. "Look at me while I touch you again, so I can see ..."

Carolyn lost herself in the pale silver world of Nick's eyes.

Nick said, "I'm ravenous."

"Let's order something from room service. You can hide in here. You won't even have to get dressed," Carolyn said. She handed Nick the room service menu and studied it over Nick's shoulder.

"I wonder what they'd think," Nick said in a suggestive tone, "if all we ordered was a bowl of whipped cream."

"That's not a particularly nutritious dinner," Carolyn said.

"I wasn't thinking of eating it ... for dinner."

Carolyn gaped and blushed, then shrieked when Nick tackled and pinned her. They wrestled and tickled and made love again. Carolyn felt lazy and satisfied when she called in their order. Nick's *sotto voce* suggestions about whipped cream and breadsticks made Carolyn blush again, but she did not order either of them.

9

Resoluto

Alison sighed and shut her magazine. She'd been waiting for Carolyn to come back to the hotel for almost two hours. The concierge had assured her the Rome dinner hour was over by now which meant that Carolyn was probably going to some infernal symphony. Alison hoped she wasn't with the conductor. Some chance. Alison had been telling herself for the last half an hour that she was a fool.

What had possessed her to cross continents? A couple of letters with uncertainty in them? Why, now that she had made it to her destination, exhausted and hungry, was she sitting in a hotel lobby, waiting for the sight of Carolyn? Love stinks, she thought. Love is the pits. Love is killing me. Love is the worst thing that has ever happened to me. Why am I putting myself through this?

Disgusted, she tucked the boring magazine in her satchel and headed for the elevator. She'd order room service, take a long, hot shower, and leave a message for Carolyn to call her in the morning.

Her stomach growled appreciatively as the elevator filled with the aroma of whatever delightful concoction was under the various domes on the room service cart next to her. Alison saw the waiter glance at her, so she smiled and rubbed her stomach to mimic hunger. When she raised her eyebrows and indicated the domes, he rattled off a list that meant nothing to her. She peered at the bill, hoping to recognize a few words so she would know what to order, but nothing made sense — except the name and room number! Vincense, room eight-one-seven. What a dope she was — Carolyn had been in her room all along. The hotel must have rung the wrong room when she had first tried.

Alison got off the elevator with the waiter and walked slowly down the long hallway while the waiter went in the opposite direction. She imagined she heard Carolyn's soft voice as the waiter was admitted into the room and reappeared a few moments later. She kept walking, hoping she didn't run out of hallway before the elevator came. She did. So she fumbled in her satchel as if looking for keys, then, mercifully, the elevator came and took the waiter away.

She virtually skipped back to Carolyn's door, then rapped as the waiter had. Grinning, she bent her head away from the peephole, and when Carolyn's voice queried her purpose, Alison faked a very bad Italian accent and said there was a problem with the order.

"It's fine," Carolyn answered.

"No, ah, reelee Signorina, I must, ah, check the order." Alison realized she sounded like Maurice Chevalier, but Carolyn opened the door.

"Surprise!" Alison swept inside and gave Carolyn a bear hug. Poor thing's in shock, she thought, when Carolyn went rigid and stayed rigid. Alison let go of her and stepped back, then realized Carolyn was wearing a hotel bathrobe.

"Did I get you out of the shower?" Alison thought she must have because Carolyn looked so odd — her face was draining of color.

Time didn't seem to move for a few moments while Carolyn stared at Alison, who stared back. Alison inhaled deeply, recognizing the smell of the food on the room service cart, and then something else — familiar, intimate. She looked around the room, and at the closed door that must lead to the bedroom. The light was on and a shadow crossed it, visible under the door.

Alison looked back at Carolyn who began to flush. Her color deepened while Alison stared at her accusingly. "I have interrupted something, haven't I?" Carolyn nodded. "I thought you were going to avoid another holiday fling. At least that's what you said in your letters."

"Ally, I have to tell you something —"

"No, you don't. Really. I don't want to know." Alison stepped backward, fumbling for the door. "None of my business."

"But it's not what you think," Carolyn said, her voice high with distress. "I mean, it is, but it's not."

"Leave me a message when you'll be free. I'm only here a couple of days," Alison said. This was her worst nightmare — it wasn't even a nightmare she'd ever had. To find Carolyn like this ... to see her after making love had been a dear fantasy, but not after someone else had been loving her! She had to get out.

The bedroom door opened and a man stood there in pants and shirt. Of course, Alison thought bitterly, the conductor.

"Carolyn, is something wrong?" The voice was not very deep, but it resonated.

"No. Nick, uh," Carolyn's voice died away, then steadied. "Nick, I want you to meet my ... dearest friend and my agent, Alison McNamara."

Nick didn't leave the doorway, but said across the semi-darkness, "A pleasure."

"Likewise," Alison said, knowing her voice dripped sarcasm she couldn't cover. She felt betrayed and wounded, as if Carolyn had thrust a long dagger right into her heart. She struck back in pain. "Is he better than your ex-husband?"

"Alison," Carolyn whispered. "I said I have something to tell you. It's not what you think."

Alison laughed at the irony. "Then I'd like to know what it is."

The conductor moved into the room. "Since you're Carolyn's dearest ... friend, though I can't say you act like it, I guess you should know the truth."

Alison stared as the light shone brightly on the conductor's face, illuminating angular features made harsher by expression than by their own design. Short hair — very Laurie Anderson. The light captured what should not have been filling a man's shirt, the points of soft breasts. Alison gasped and caught her stomach in raw pain. This was worse, so much worse.

"Alison," Carolyn said, "Nick is a woman. I'm ... I'm a lesbian."

"No," Alison whispered. Men she could forgive, maybe. Men she could compete with, knowing that they would never be emotionally sustaining to Carolyn. But another woman ... a powerful, daring *butch* woman ... no. She groped for the door, and put her hand on the knob.

"Alison, please don't go," Carolyn pleaded. "Not like this. I've been hoping you could accept me."

"A friend wouldn't leave like this," the conductor said. "Carolyn obviously cares for you, so why are you hurting her?"

"I didn't travel thousands of miles to see this," Alison said.

"See what?" The conductor's contempt cut into Alison.

Alison whirled around. She would not go home whipped by this ... this bulldyke! "To see my best friend making a fool of herself over a predatory bitch!"

Carolyn gasped. "Alison, you don't know what you're saying."

The conductor laughed and walked toward Alison, stopping near enough for Alison to see and smell the traces of lovemaking that hadn't yet been washed away. Her world shattered.

"I've been called a lot of things, but never predatory."

"You're a woman so afraid of her womanhood you're hiding it, lying and making Carolyn lie, too. You dress like a man because you can't be a woman. You're not strong enough to be a woman!"

"I assure you, I'm a woman. Carolyn can attest to it."

The conductor knows, Alison thought. She shut her eyes to block out the conductor's triumphant gleam as the brutal truth sank into Alison. She knows I'm in love with Carolyn. But Carolyn can't know. Please let me save at least that much of my dignity.

"A shadow-woman, then," Alison said weakly.

"Alison, don't," Carolyn said, her voice thick with tears.

She pities me. "I don't need your mercy," Alison said. "I guess I'll cut my stay short."

She evaded the hand that would have caught her arm, closed her ears to Carolyn's plea, and scrambled out the door. She ran the length of the corridor to the service stairs and stumbled down the two flights to her room.

She hadn't really unpacked — what had she been thinking, that she and Carolyn would share a room? *Stupid, I'm so stupid.* She ignored the phone when it started to ring. *Keeping my life on hold, waiting for her — it's over.* Cases stuffed, she fled the room, threw her credit card down at the front desk, then flung herself into a cab.

The darkness was filled with the conductor's triumphant face. She tried to make the image go away, but it persisted. She could ruin Nicolas Frost if she wanted to, she told herself. She could *out* Nicolas Frost with a vengeance! What a story — hey world press, he's a she and she's a dyke!

She rocked back into the depths of the cab. She couldn't do it. It would hurt Carolyn, and even though Alison wanted, at this moment, to hurt Carolyn the way she herself was hurting, she knew she couldn't do that to another lesbian. But if Nicolas Frost hurt Carolyn, or ever said anything homophobic, then nothing would stop her.

The next flight to Frankfurt left in an hour. Alison went to the women's restroom to wait, sobbing silently in huddled misery. She wore her sunglasses on the plane, and knew they would not fool anyone.

♥

Nick held Carolyn against her, knowing Carolyn was hardly aware of her. She was ashamed of herself, but hoped that in the long run the nasty scene would teach Carolyn a vital lesson — the world did not like them. Nick wasn't ashamed of being a lesbian, but she wanted too much from the world to risk her standing. Carolyn would learn that if her best friend couldn't accept her, then very few people would. She had sensed, deep down, that Alison was in love with Carolyn, but she still didn't regret what she'd done. If Alison didn't have the courage to tell Carolyn, then Nick wasn't going to do it for her.

"Carolyn, you're going to make yourself sick," Nick said. "Come to bed and try to calm down."

"I can't," she said between ragged breaths. "Alison has always been there for me. After my parents died, after that awful marriage, Alison was there. She's like my sister ... she sells my books, she made this trip possible ..." Carolyn began to cry again.

Later, when Carolyn slept fitfully, tucked under Nick's arm, Nick dreamed of a perfect world where she and Carolyn shared breakfast every day, where Carolyn was always in the conductor's box, and Carolyn was there to be loved and to love her every night. She dreamed of a perfect world where the premiere conductor and world-famous author stood side-by-side for photographs that were captioned, "Nicola Frost and Carolyn Vincense, long-time companions." Maybe someday she would be as open as Martina Navratilova. She had hoped the masquerade would be over soon, but this recording deal would lead to others. The dream would have to wait for a few more years, but someday she would be too established to oust. She would make waiting worth Carolyn's while. She yawned and drowsed, smiling in the darkness. She could make dreams come true with one wave of her baton.

The next few days in Rome were heaven for Nick. The performances seemed less quarrelsome, the weather stayed sultry and Carolyn did not want to get out of bed. They were both starving all the time but food was low on the priority list. On the day before Carolyn was due to leave for California, Nick arrived back at her suite to find her having tea with Oscar. She had obviously been shopping because Nick would have remembered the tight Italian jeans that encased the slender legs. She would have noticed the shirt, too — crinkled white cotton with a rose splashed over one breast and a long stem that twined its way to the hem of the shirt which missed meeting the top of the jeans by a couple of centimeters. The sight of Carolyn's lightly tanned midriff made Nick wobbly. Ordinarily she would have minded being wobbly, but she didn't care in the least as she dropped a kiss on the mouth that curved in welcome. Carolyn caught her and kissed her back, taking her time.

"Ahem," Oscar said.

Nick broke off the kiss long enough to say, "Not my fault."

"Really?" Oscar sighed heavily and made a sound of unmistakable British distaste when Nick went back to kissing Carolyn. "The least you could do is retire to the bedroom."

"Good idea," Carolyn said into Nick's mouth.

"Disgusting," Nick heard Oscar say as they closed the door behind them.

Nick immediately slid her hands under the shirt. Her fingers trembled over the golden skin of Carolyn's stomach. She was considerably weakened when Carolyn pulled the shirt over her head. Still, she had the strength to unhook Carolyn's bra and kiss the red marks the straps had left. Her hands captured the heavy softness the bra had cradled. "Torture trap," she murmured.

"Taking it off this way is so much nicer than doing it by myself," Carolyn said. Her back arched and Nick hugged Carolyn to her, her hands massaging the smooth skin of Carolyn's back. Her hands appreciated the snug fit of the jeans over Carolyn's derriere. Then Carolyn pushed her back on the bed.

"Don't I get to undress?"

"When I say so," Carolyn said, her lips curving in a sensuous smile.

"Are you going to have your way with me?" Nick's hands returned to Carolyn's breasts as Carolyn leaned over her.

"*Sí.* Right-o. *Oui. Ja.* You betcha."

"Good answer." Nick shuddered as Carolyn's hand pressed against her crotch. She unzipped her pants with a moan. She could feel how wet she was now, and she knew how eagerly Carolyn's fingers would take her.

Carolyn's fingers were quick and sure. Nick gasped, meeting Carolyn's rhythm. "So ... fast. *Vivace.*" Carolyn's hand stopped, then moved so slowly Nick groaned.

"No, *largo*," Carolyn murmured.

"Who's the conductor here?" Her mouth was dry. Her hips arched frantically.

Carolyn pushed Nick's shirt up and stripped away the gauze, her mouth tasting Nick's breasts the moment they were bare.

Nick groaned deep in her throat. She could think of nothing but offering her body to Carolyn and succumbing to the way Carolyn gave her pleasure.

For some reason Nick's brain kept reminding her that it was the middle of the afternoon, that Oscar was probably still in the next room, but her body didn't care.

Carolyn's body apparently didn't care either. The softness Nick's mouth found was beyond words — beyond music even. And the sweetness that Nick's tongue explored was the essence of Carolyn's passion, heady and addictive.

Nick said later, "I suppose we should get some supper."

"Umm." Carolyn sighed and curled herself around Nick's body. Nick felt new wetness against her hip. She had thought herself utterly satisfied, but her body responded to Carolyn's wetness with its own. When Carolyn finally let her out of the bed she raided the fruit basket sent by the hotel for strawberries and a banana.

"Toss me an apple," Carolyn said. She sat up, pulling a sheet up over her breasts. Nick smiled to herself. Carolyn's usual modesty was at odds with her incredible passion. On the other hand, Nick was already fantasizing about removing the sheet and tasting Carolyn's breasts again.

"I don't want to go home, Nick, not yet." Carolyn studied her apple after she bit into it.

Nick's heart did a jig. She had deliberately not brought up Carolyn's scheduled departure, waiting for some sign from Carolyn about what she wanted. "What do you want to do?"

Carolyn stared up at Nick, then her gaze fell, riveting on the triangle of hair between Nick's legs. Nick swayed. "I want to keep on making love to you. And I know I'm not ready to face home."

"Come home with me then. London has more museums than you can count. And musty churches by the score. You'll love it."

"Okay." Carolyn set down her half-eaten apple. Nick swayed again when Carolyn said huskily, "Come back over here."

Nick told her legs not to open again but they did it all by themselves. Really, it was getting embarrassing. But she could live with it.

♥

Alison was aware that Devon was watching her, but she did not meet his gaze, or anyone else's for that matter. He could stare. She knew she'd made a fool of herself. She did not want his pity. She paid someone else to water Carolyn's lawn, but otherwise her life went on. Nothing had changed except a future that hadn't been hers anyway. And she had a lot of work to do, filling in a big hole in her business now that a major client was no longer there.

Sacramento's spring was in full glory. Alison had considered living in the Bay Area, but spring was her favorite season, and Sacramento's frosty winters faded into a cool, green thaw followed by weeks of wonderful spring. The ballfield grass went from slate-green to a verdant carpet of life. Along the sidewalks azalea bushes replaced dark winter leaves with vivid scarlet and violet flowers, and the delicate tips of daffodil bulbs cracked the soil in window boxes, and gardens put forth blazing yellow, peach and white blooms. The freeways were a delight to drive, lined with purple and red carpets of ice plant and divided by rows of rejoicing oleander bushes. The season of rebirth and new surprises went on for weeks, slowly easing into the hot summer. It had been a beautiful spring. Alison couldn't remember when she had been more depressed.

The window box outside her office offered two neglected irises and several tulips, and Alison opened the window to give them some water. Poor plants, she shouldn't take her depression out on them. The soil rewarded her with a puff of mulchy aroma, the smell of something living. When she turned back, Devon was just laying an envelope on her desk, and he left without his usual jabs and sarcasm — it was air mail from Rome. Alison thought about reading it then and there, but her composure couldn't risk it. It was only later that evening, after she'd finished a lonely Canadian Club on the rocks, that she finally read Carolyn's letter.

Dear Alison:

I've given you some time to think and maybe by now you can better accept the new me. I'm sorry you found out that way, but when I began to accept how I was changing I planned to tell you anyway — I couldn't go through my life without sharing my changes with you. And I'm very sorry you left, because I think we would have had a lot of fun traveling together. The new me shouldn't affect our friendship, but of course I know it will. I feel toward you as I always have and so how much our friendship changes is up to you. I hope you can accept me. I hope you can accept how my life is going to change. I suppose on a business level I

*should tell you I doubt Carly Vincent will pen
another book. She's dead ... but Carolyn Vincense is
finally alive.*

*I've decided for now to return home with Nick to
London. I don't know how long I'll stay. Au revoir.*

Carolyn

Alison read the letter again. She hadn't thought
about what she'd do when Carolyn returned. She
hadn't realized, until now, that she still had to come
out to Carolyn. It was simply awful that she'd left
Carolyn with the impression she was homophobic, for
God's sake. But she still had to decide how much
she would tell Carolyn about how she felt.

And how did she feel? As dead as Carly Vincent.
And without enough emotion in her entire body to
grieve. It seemed natural to call Sam and perfectly
all right to accept Sam's invitation to coffee so
Alison could tell her about her trip.

But as she sat with the cup of coffee in her
hand, Alison couldn't find the words to tell Sam
what had happened. Her throat filled with an
asteroid-sized lump. Sam, sitting across from Alison
at the memorable coffee table, reached over and took
the cup away. Then, when Alison found she couldn't
manage a coherent sentence, Sam moved next to her
and rocked Alison against her shoulder. Sam said
everything would be o-k.

Alison was overwhelmed with images of Carolyn
making love with the conductor. Her hands fumbled
with Sam's shirt. Then Sam undressed her and
murmured in Alison's ear, "Call it comfort for now."

♥

In the West End of London, on a narrow street where the three-story residences were all identical, right down to the window boxes, Carolyn waited patiently for Nick to unlock the door to her flat. Nick grinned when the key turned and the door swung back. "My castle, only two flights up. After you."

Carolyn had not known what to expect, but the drama of the flat was entirely in keeping with the drama of Nick. The yellowed linoleum floor was almost hidden by thick rugs in striking black and red geometric patterns. The small living room was dominated by Mondrian prints illuminated by several precisely focused track lights. Nick pressed switches and more light sprang from art deco sconces mounted on the walls at about hip height.

"The torchieres were here when I moved in. I've changed the fabric on the wall, though," Nick said. "Decorating absorbed quite a bit of spare energy after I donned my male garb. It was actually a challenge to find a scheme that was neither masculine or feminine."

"It's very like you, somehow." Carolyn ran one hand over the jacquard pattern of white on white that was tucked and folded around the torchieres. She wondered how her own home looked, now that Samantha had probably finished it. The thought brought other images of home and with a twinge, she recalled Alison. The void she could feel inside was one reason she had delayed her return home.

"That door's to the other bedroom — my music library and instruments are in there. Come give our bedroom a look-see," Nick said, dragging suitcases with her.

"I can hardly wait." Between their flights, performances, sightseeing and Carolyn's period they hadn't made love for four whole days. She was sure this feeling of wanting sex every minute of every day — or so it seemed — would fade in time, but she wasn't in any hurry. She was mildly worried about her feelings for Nick being entirely too much on a physical level ... but the worry was very easy to ignore.

The bedroom had more of the same black and red decor, with modern art prints, but Carolyn didn't focus on them. She jumped over the pile of suitcases with a whoop. Nick turned just in time to catch Carolyn and they tumbled onto the bed.

Carolyn's fingers found their way under Nick's jacket, then under her shirt. She teased the nipples she knew were under the gauze. Carolyn's fingers were getting very skilled at finding them. Right ... there.

Nick sighed as Carolyn continued her teasing. "You have a one-track mind."

Alarmed, Carolyn looked up at Nick's expression. "Shall I stop?" She realized that Nick looked very tired. They'd left directly from a matinee concert for the airport. The journey had really been no further than Los Angeles to Seattle, but Customs had been a trial. Her fingers captured the swelling tips. "They're undecided, but I think they want me to go on."

"I want you to go on, too, but I want a shower. Heathrow was an armpit."

Carolyn smirked. "I think I'll take a shower with you."

"Lecher," Nick said fondly. She went to a bare wall, pressed in on the fabric, and a door appeared out of the jacquard print.

Carolyn laughed. "I hope I can find that during the night."

"It's so French Renaissance, isn't it? I think of *Liaisons Dangereuses* and *The Three Musketeers* every time I use it."

Carolyn followed Nick into the more prosaically decorated bathroom. The shower was over an old-fashioned tub with massive claw feet and porcelain taps. "I love this tub. It could be rather fun for two."

"Don't bet on it," Nick said. "When I want a bath I have to heat water. The hot water in this flat is sporadic at best. It pays to plan on showering quickly."

Carolyn warbled "Mandy" as she showered, accompanied by Nick's groans of protest. The hot water abruptly ceased, and Nick howled with laughter as Carolyn swore and stumbled out of the tub. Nick was wrapped in a man's large robe that hung on the back of the door. She nudged a suitcase with her foot. "We're going to have to find a place for you to hang your clothes. Your robe is in there somewhere."

"Let's share yours for now," Carolyn suggested.

Nick turned around, a relaxed and happy smile on her face. She opened her robe and Carolyn snuggled inside it. "You may always share my robe."

Afterwards, when Nick was breathing steadily and deeply, Carolyn stared at the dark ceiling. She wondered what Alison was doing. The fact that she wondered, with the taste of Nick still in her mouth, bothered her. It took a long time to fall asleep.

♥

"I heard from Carolyn," Alison said. She had received a postcard from London simply saying Carolyn was having fun and would be home soon. Carolyn wanted, it seemed, to go on as if nothing had changed. Sam turned over in bed, her body moving a little farther away. "She's having fun in London."

"I didn't know she went on to London. What's there?"

"Her new lover," Alison said quietly.

"So that's what went wrong," Sam said. "I've been patiently waiting for you to tell me."

"Sam, I'm sorry. I brought it up because that's what I want to say to you. I'm sorry, so sorry."

"After last night and last Tuesday, and after the game Saturday — you're sorry? I'm not."

"I'm using you. I feel like a total jerk."

"I meant what I said about comfort." Sam's voice was gentle and sincere.

"But you're hoping for more." She looked over at Sam's calm face. "I don't think you should do that."

Sam's expression didn't alter. "When it comes to controlling who we love and how we love them, you're not exactly the best advisor, sweetie." She smiled faintly.

Alison could only nod at the truth of Sam's

statement. "I've been thinking about what I'll do when she comes back. I have to come out to her — I can't let her go on thinking I reacted the way I did because I'm homophobic or something. And the only way to explain myself is to tell her I've been lusting after her for years. That's the part I'm having trouble with."

"And you still feel the same way?"

Alison slowly shook her head and Sam's eyebrows raised slightly. "No, I don't feel the same way at all. Now I love her."

"You loved her before."

"I loved a china doll in a shop window. I acted like a child because someone else touched it. I didn't love Carolyn, I loved unrequited love, and all the excuses it gave me for not making permanent attachments to people. Including you. She . . . she was my straight-woman shield."

Sam's gaze dropped and fixed on a point somewhere near Alison's earlobe. "I think I understand where you're going with this, but truly, I'm not sure you know your own mind, not yet."

"But I do, Sam. She scares me to death now that I know I could be with her if she wanted me. That postcard put my heart rate up to about two hundred. I was always in control before. I could have told her how I felt at any time, but I pretended it was her fault I couldn't come out to her." Alison laughed ironically. "I loved a Carolyn that didn't exist. And now I see her as another lesbian, a full-grown adult — and I love this new woman. I never really loved the old Carolyn because I never trusted her. But now I do. Now I have to tell her how I feel. I have to accept her answer."

Sam cleared her throat. "That part's not particularly easy." Alison put her hand on Sam's shoulder, but Sam was rolling out of bed. "Want some breakfast?"

"I'm sorry, Sam."

Sam looked back as she put on her robe. Alison had a feeling it was the last time she would see Sam's dark body in all its gorgeous nakedness. "I'm sorry, too. But I'm a big girl. There are other f-i-s-h in the sea," she said, her philosophical tone at odds with overly bright eyes and smile.

"And better fish, too." While Sam was in the bathroom, Alison quickly dressed. She took up the question of breakfast with false cheer and appetite, and they got through muffins and coffee somehow. Sam was smiling when Alison finally left, without a kiss goodbye.

♥

Carolyn bent over the score Nick was studying at the piano in the second bedroom. Four violins were carefully wrapped on shelves, along with a lute, a collection of harmonicas and a saxophone. Otherwise, the room was stuffed with sheet-music-laden shelves. Only the area around the piano was reasonably ordered. Carolyn brushed away the crumbs her crumpet had dropped on the keys when she bit into it. Toast done on one side ... it was weird, but it was food. She liked the Seville orange marmalade that Nick smeared on her crumpets and scones, but the thought of an Egg McMuffin made her stomach rumble.

"So tell me about this little number you're recording." Carolyn smiled innocently at Nick's narrowed gaze.

"This little number has over six hundred performers."

"Like the USC Trojans Marching band, right?"

Carolyn didn't get the expected rise out of Nick. Nick said, her eyes wide with consideration, "A marching band version of Mahler, now there's a thought."

Carolyn realized she was being teased and asked Nick to show her how an orchestral score was read. She'd had a few years of piano lessons and knew which way was up, but these sheets were a bewildering mass of staves and notes.

Nick traced notes on the score with one hand, while her other chose chords or rippled out melody lines to illustrate her point. She sang the melody line in a steady contralto while her hands demonstrated percussion and string work on the piano. "So while the violins are playing this melody and holding this note, the kettle drums come in softly and it lingers while the oboe comes in, then the choir ... slowly, like this." She played the page over again, vocalizing the effects of the kettle drum and oboe. "So you have boom wait wait wait hand hand and wait." Her finger punched the page at the corresponding bunch of notes. Carolyn was speechless with laughter by the time Nick finished the next page. Nick looked at her in mock disdain. "There's nothing funny about it. This is my craft."

"Do you make such funny noises in front of the musicians?"

"I only make funny noises for you," Nick said. Her smile softened and Carolyn saw her swallow.

"Nick," Carolyn said, putting her crumpet down, "you're never going to get any work done if you keep looking at me like that."

"Like what?" Nick didn't protest as Carolyn pulled Nick's sweatshirt up.

"It's the look you get when you want me to ... you know," Carolyn said, her face burning. "And when you look like that I immediately want to." She spun the piano stool around, bracing Nick against the piano. Her hands slipped down Nick's sweatpants and then she pressed Nick back against the piano rack where the Mahler score was spread.

"We're wrinkling the music," Nick murmured.

"Mahler's dead. He won't care." They slid to the floor together amidst a shower of music sheets.

Later, Carolyn helped Nick smooth out the crumpled paper. Just to ensure the sanctity of the score, Carolyn decided it would be best if she continued her scheduled tour of the British Museum and left Nick to study in peace for the day.

She was unfocused as she meandered from exhibit to exhibit and from building to building. She found herself in a special exhibit of goddess figurines which included a lifesize simulation of how the agrarian goddess-worshippers might have built their homes. The exhibit was sparsely attended and Carolyn thought she was alone until she stepped into the room marked SHRINE. She surprised two women who were fervently embracing.

The women sprang apart, looking everywhere but at Carolyn. Carolyn cleared her throat and said, "So sorry. Uh, I think I'm the only one in here and I'm leaving." Even as she backed out of the room the two women were moving together again.

Carolyn's pulse was racing. It seemed now that all of the other people attending the exhibit were women. Had she by accident wandered into a lesbian equivalent of a gym or bar? Was this how lesbians met? She looked around again, surreptitiously examining the other women. She was appalled at her incredibly explicit sexual fantasies as she looked at each body, but she couldn't help herself — it felt too natural. The whole experience somehow made her stronger inside.

When she left the exhibit area she noticed a tall, raven-haired woman walking toward her. There was only a superficial resemblance to Alison, but it was too late — her heart had leapt, she was already smiling in welcome. The elegant woman looked at Carolyn with a frown of disapproval, drawing her coat around her as if to say, "How dare you think I'm one of you."

Carolyn colored furiously and hurried away. The woman's response bothered her, but her own reactions when she had thought of Alison disturbed her more. It was obvious she had feelings for Alison that she had never examined closely enough. It was also obvious that her feelings for Nick had not supplanted these hidden longings for Alison. She had wanted to come to London with Nick, but if she was going to be frank with herself, she hadn't wanted it nearly as much as she had wanted to put off going home.

Carolyn wandered back to Nick's flat, taking enough time to allow an afternoon appointment — a student sent to Nick by another conductor for appraisal — to come and go. Nick was ready to relax when Carolyn climbed the stairs.

"So was the violinist the new Perlman?"

"Not hardly," Nick said. "I was brutal."

"Oh dear," Carolyn said. "I could never do it. I'd feel so sorry for them."

"Don't feel sorry for the boy wonder," Nick said. "I was brutal, but I had to be. If I raved I'd be irresponsible. Hard work makes the difference, not my opinion. He wouldn't give it up if I told him to, but if I encouraged too much he might stop working. He'll need all the hard work he can muster." Nick smiled. "I certainly couldn't have told him he plays the violin better than I do."

Carolyn laughed and ruffled Nick's hair. She liked it with a little curl, and she admitted to herself she was starting to feel uncomfortable about the deception the slicked-back style symbolized.

They had a quiet dinner out and then went to a jazz club Nick liked. When Carolyn stumbled sleepily into bed she heard a rustling sound in the bed.

"What on earth?"

Nick's voice laughed softly in the darkness. "After the effect the Mahler score had on you, I thought I'd try Bach. I hope you like the fugues."

Carolyn loved fugues. They traded point and counterpoint well into the night.

"Come on, doll, I'm going to be late," Nick called.

Carolyn emerged from the bedroom, her face flushed as she rushed to get her coat and step into shoes. "And whose fault is it? I already dressed once this morning!"

"Women," Nick said. She was pleased with the morning's extracurricular activities. "It takes so long for you to get yourselves together."

Carolyn favored Nick with a slitted, intense glance that hid the robin's-egg blue Nick was so fond of. "Ha ha," she snapped.

"Sorry, love." Nick opened the door while Carolyn gathered a small satchel containing a book, notebook and sightseeing guide. She wondered what had made Carolyn so touchy lately.

They took a cab to Covent Garden and Nick forgot about Carolyn's flash of ill-humor as she transformed into a hyper-tourist, demanding that Nick name every landmark and point out anybody at all who was remotely famous.

"Okay, okay, just don't embarrass me by gawking," Nick said, laughing.

Carolyn took mock-offense, saying, "I never gawk. I may stare, but I never gawk. Nor, I might add, am I ever *agog*." Nick pointed out a famous coloratura who was headed away from them toward the smaller rehearsal studios. "I love her voice," Carolyn said, sighing. "Okay, I'm agog."

"Gee, I never made you agog."

"No, but you made me just about everything else."

Grinning, Nick pulled Carolyn along to the large hall, the only one that could possibly accommodate the performers for the *Symphony of a Thousand.* Thousand was an overstatement, but six hundred and fifty performers were not easily staged. "See, it's a fairly boring concert hall. You'll get tired of it in three minutes."

"So I see. And you can hardly wait to get to work. I can take a hint. Well, I guess I'm going to go poking and prodding into more famous places, darling. Musty palaces today." Carolyn held up her mouth for a kiss then waved as she headed back on the aisle.

Nick watched her walk away. She could not believe her good fortune. In the hall, a rapidly growing knot of people gathered at the foot of the stage. Her life was too ... too good. But she was realistic enough to expect the other shoe to drop. Still, as long as she had Carolyn, she could survive anything.

♥

Carolyn arrived back at the flat tired but pleased. From a fine art poster shop she had purchased prints she thought would match the color scheme she and Sam had discussed. The color was almost irrelevant — both prints were of Mary Cassatt's most modern works and Carolyn had always liked them the best.

She stopped short in surprise as she realized she

was not alone — Oscar was perched in one of the chairs as if waiting for someone.

"I hope I did not startle you," he said. "I called out, but I doubt you could have heard me over the rustling of your parcels."

"And the sound of my own pounding heart," Carolyn added as she went into the bedroom to drop her bags. "Two flights of stairs — in Sacramento, that's two good reasons to put in an elevator." She cast herself down on the divan. "Pure laziness, that's why so many of us Americans are pudgy."

"Pudgy? An interesting colloquialism," Oscar said.

After a few moment's silence, Carolyn sat up and said, "Why do I think you have something unpleasant to discuss?" Oscar usually looked completely at ease, but at the moment he was tapping one finger on the arm of the chair — for him, he was positively fidgeting.

"My dear, I will admit right out that in my life I have liked very few women. I worked with many talented women, and I have admired and supported many more. But I rarely liked them. I'm not absolutely sure I would say I liked Nicolas."

Carolyn noted that even when they were alone, Oscar referred to Nick by her full masculine name. "Meaning what?"

"That I must simply say I like you. You are an unassuming, refreshingly intelligent woman. Therefore, what I must also say is difficult."

Carolyn was not very good at confrontation ... but she had new strength, and she thought she knew what Oscar was leading up to. It was nothing she hadn't been stewing over herself for the last day or two. "You want to know if I'm serious and if I've thought through all the consequences of being Nick's girlfriend."

Oscar smiled slightly. "As I said, intelligent. I have nurtured Nick through the years and don't wish to see them wasted. She is on the very edge, the brink of all her dreams, and mine."

"And how does my being in her life change that?"

"It's not you, my dear. It's a successful relationship. The edge of Nick's drive is her will to overcome."

"So she must be unhappy and alone to be successful?"

"No," Oscar said gravely. "But I believe she is convinced she is invincible now. She believes she can flaunt you under the noses of people she will later need, and they won't mind. She has really only told one lie, until a few weeks ago."

Carolyn sighed. "I know that right now I'm enjoying a tiny window in her life that isn't quite as much of an uproar as the rest. I also know that I don't have what it takes to wait with her. I'm only now realizing how much she wants it all — fame and success and then acknowledgment as a woman. Nothing but all of those things will satisfy her." And it had been easy, she wanted to say, easy to not look forward.

"And it frightens you?"

"Not so much frightens as intimidates. I'm not the one to help her achieve those things — I know I'm a distraction. But I also know that for now I'm making her happy and vice versa." For now. But if she looked forward ... well, she'd written enough books to know an ending when she saw one.

"I don't believe that Nicolas feels this is temporary."

"I know," Carolyn said. Nick had begun referring to the flat as "our" flat and making other comments that added up to permanence. Carolyn had been trying to find a way to head her off. "I'm not going to lead her on, if that's what you wanted to know."

"I didn't think you would, my dear, not consciously."

Carolyn looked up as Oscar stood. She said, "I suppose I should be angry that you're interfering in something not your concern."

"I know that Nicolas would tell me to mind my own business in not so polite terms."

"Since you like me, I suppose you'll have to trust me." She followed him to the stairs. "I want Nick to have her dreams — if she had to choose between me and her dreams, well, I don't flatter myself that she'd even hesitate."

"I left off one reason why I like you." Oscar turned from the top of the stair, and put one finger under Carolyn's chin. "You are sensible."

Carolyn frowned. "Hardly a romantic trait."

"But a valuable one. I can see myself out. I'm hoping to catch Nick before the end of rehearsal."

Carolyn watched after him until she heard the click of the door at the bottom of the stairs. She thought about what he had said — it didn't make her feel anything but sad. She didn't want this time with Nick to end. And even as that thought crossed her mind, she knew it was already ending. She suddenly wanted to cry, but Nick would notice and Carolyn was just not ready to tell Nick why.

To distract herself, Carolyn looked through the books she purchased from a women's bookstore near Picadilly Circus. In the back had been a section labeled "Womyn/Womyn." Her recollection of *Publisher's Weekly* reviews had helped her pick out a couple of titles, and the clerk had recommended several more she probably wouldn't be able to find in the States.

She'd never paid more than peripheral attention to the reviews on books from women's presses — she had a lot of time to make up for. There was probably a bookstore near home where she could continue to stock up and learn about the history of her newfound sexuality. Home. Even without Alison, and maybe because of Alison, she had to go back.

"You're a beautiful sight. Missed you," Nick said, after she bounded up the stairs an hour later. She kissed Carolyn lightly, then headed for the bedroom, ruffling her slicked-down hair into curls. "I'm going to take a quick shower. Think about what you want to do tonight."

Carolyn listened to the water running and thought about what she wanted to do. She wanted to go to a lesbian place. It didn't matter what kind of place, as long as it was lesbians only. She knew they couldn't with Nick dressed as a man ... she'd be recognized by someone. She'd seen three women in masculine clothes at the bookstore, but their attire was a declaration. To Carolyn they had seemed the antithesis of Nick. Nick didn't use the masculine part of her nature to express herself as a woman and lesbian, she buried her womanhood in it, waiting. It would erupt someday, but until then — Carolyn was beginning to wonder why Nick wasn't crazy from the strain of playing such a thorough charade.

"The concert and choirmasters are top-drawer." Nick threw her robed body down on the sofa as she toweled her hair. "This is going to be a good recording."

"Don't discount the contribution of the top-drawer conductor," Carolyn said.

"You're good for my ego," Nick said. She fell over, head finding a pillow. "Wake me in thirty minutes," she said sleepily.

Carolyn smiled fondly. Soft legs and the curve of one breast were not quite covered by the large terry cloth robe. She returned to her book, aware that today could be a pattern for a lifetime — not that Nick's life would ever be totally patterned. And the more famous she became, the less privacy they would have and the more constricted their lifestyle would be. How could she have books with "lesbian" in the title around the house? How could she be a lesbian anywhere except in bed? Why didn't that seem like enough? Nick would thrive on all of it, while Carolyn knew it was the last kind of existence she wanted.

And she knew that explaining her feelings to Nick would be hard on both of them. She had to find the right opportunity and the right words. She waited the appointed thirty minutes, then woke Nick with a kiss that left no doubt as to what Carolyn wanted to do with the evening. Leaving would be easier if only her body didn't respond so eagerly to Nick's touch.

10
Coda; Da Capo al Segno

Carolyn looked down at the Great Salt Lake, then collapsed back in her seat. Almost home. Even the headset blaring out the inane in-flight movie didn't give her any escape from the memory of Nick's silent suffering. She had hoped her careful, gentle announcement wouldn't hit Nick too hard. But it had. She relived the scene over and over.

They'd gone dancing and met some people Nick knew. Nick introduced Carolyn as her girlfriend —

and that was the moment Carolyn had realized she couldn't let it go on. She couldn't submerge herself to the point of putting Nick's masquerade before her burgeoning self-confidence and esteem. And she saw what Oscar meant, that Nick couldn't afford to lie so boldly. Some things people wouldn't forgive. She knew Nick felt different, so, later, when they were alone, she'd tried to be gentle. She'd tried to explain that Nick's life couldn't encompass Carolyn too, not now. Nick had too much to lose.

"Well, let me bloody well bother about that," Nick had retorted. "I love you."

Even now, Carolyn was seeing Nick's face again. Three little words ... uttered with such conviction that Carolyn had been flooded with guilt. "Nick, don't," she had said before she could help herself.

Nick had frozen. "Well that's that," she said finally.

"I have to go home."

"Of course you do. I was a fool to think otherwise."

"I'm very fond of you —"

"Please don't." One hand slashed the air, silencing Carolyn. "I obviously misread the situation."

Carolyn had found it very hard to find her voice. "Nothing is turning out like I thought it would. It would be so easy to pretend to be a man and a woman. But I can't pay the price."

"What price do you pay?" Nick's voice was cold and hard. "I'm the woman passing as a man."

"I couldn't be a lesbian."

"I don't know what you call what we do in bed, but I call it lesbianism."

"There's *more* than that, so much more I can

only guess at it. What we do in bed is just the tip of the iceberg," Carolyn said. "I wouldn't have thought something I never knew I was would mean so much in so little time. I want to be a lesbian, open and proud. I want to learn what that means, grow and change as I learn. I have to tell my family. You probably won't recognize me in a few years, but I've got to do it."

"Then do it. Who am I to criticize you for doing what you feel you have to do?" Nick had averted her eyes and that had been the end of the talk. They were extremely polite to each other and Nick had been very solicitous of Carolyn's well-being. She had even seen Carolyn off at the airport. Even though she understood why Nick was withdrawn, Carolyn had longed for a last word as lovers, a goodbye as lovers. The last kiss had been restrained and ended with a little moan from Nick who had murmured goodbye and walked away.

Carolyn pulled off the headset, irritated with the sexist premise of the movie. There was only one way to describe how she felt, trite though it may be: her heart was heavy. She had so much to thank Nick for — courage, passion, aspiration — and she had only ended up hurting her. She didn't want to undo one moment of her time with Nick, but she wished she could change the hurt.

"Auntie Carl, Auntie Carl." Voices squealed behind her. Carolyn wheeled around and braced herself for her two exuberant nephews. Seconds later she was sitting on the floor in the airport while her nephews crawled all over her, exclaiming over her new clothes, poking her traveling case which bulged in a way they were no doubt interpreting — correctly — as presents.

"Okay, okay, you two, give Auntie a chance to breathe," Margot said as she pulled one affectionate boy off her sister-in-law while the other eluded his mother's grasp. Carolyn laughed, overwhelmed by the show of cupboard love. "Boys, I said behave." Margot didn't raise her voice, but both sons quieted down while still favoring Carolyn with large puppy eyes that asked for treats.

Carolyn knew that as soon as the presents were distributed they'd both forget about Auntie Carl until they wanted to be tucked up and told a story. Still, it felt good to be loved, even if it was just for her souvenirs. Deep in the suitcase were the earrings she had bought for Alison; she didn't know if she'd ever get the chance to give them to her.

She said very little as Margot drove her home; she was exhausted from the day spent between countries and she didn't want to talk about what she'd done in Europe. She hadn't mentioned Nick in any of her postcards to Curt and Margot. But she planned to tell them everything, provided her courage didn't fail. If she couldn't tell her family, then why had she left Nick? She would trust the love they had always shown her.

The boys were poring over Danish picture books and sounding out the long Dutch words as Margot brought her up to date on the happenings in her family. Carolyn considered her sister-in-law. Margot was a generous, loving woman who was a barracuda when her home, husband or children were threatened. Would Margot regard Carolyn's lesbianism as a threat?

"So when are you going to show us pictures?" Margot turned the car down Carolyn's street. "Maybe Curt will decide he could handle Europe."

"As soon as they're developed. Listen, Margot, I need to talk to you and Curt about something. When do you have an evening free? It's not urgent, but . . . soon."

"How about Friday?" Margot looked at Carolyn quizzically. "You look exhausted and excited at the same time. Are we going to be talking about romance? What was that extra trip to London all about?"

"It's got something to do with romance, but trust me, Margot, you're way off. I just need to explain something."

"Come for dinner, then," Margot said.

"And tell us a story," two voices chimed from the back seat.

"Okay, okay. I'll head over around six. Thanks for the lift."

Carolyn unlocked her door, overwhelmed with thoughts of Nick and Alison, yet with a surging joy to be home again. She could already see that Sam's work was done. She eagerly pulled up the blinds, gasping as light flooded her living room.

It was completely different and she immediately loved every inch of it. Sam had worked wonders without changing the fundamental simplicity of the house. There was textured pale peach wallcovering along one long wall, and a gray-blue rug that brought out the grain in the worn oak parquet. The sofa and side chairs had been reupholstered in tweeded blue and peach and ivory and the jewel-toned tapestry Carolyn's mother had woven was now highlighted by the pale wall behind it. It was lovely and comfortable, all at the same time. The Mary Cassatt prints would look spectacular.

In a daze, Carolyn wandered to her bedroom. It featured new colors, too, and a new bed with a brass headboard that formed a love knot. Sam had worked wonders. Her office was untouched, except for new rugs on the floor that echoed colors from other rooms. The kitchen was the same, but there was a note on the refrigerator from Sam that warned her about ideas for the kitchen.

Carolyn smiled and told herself she was happy to be home. She told herself she had no regrets. New interiors, new exteriors. She had a new life to lead.

She closed all the blinds and tumbled into bed, noticing right away that the mattress was a vast improvement over the old one. The fresh sheets felt wonderful. She was glad to be back in her old room, glad to be in a place that didn't remind her of ... anything in Europe. The problem was that despite the new decor, too much of the house reminded her of Alison.

The next morning she still felt a little jet-lagged as she unpacked, did some laundry and wandered round the house. She didn't quite know what to do with herself. The silence of the house was deafening. Carolyn was watching the cup of noodles boiling in the microwave when something inside her snapped. She opened the door, heedless of the hot liquid bubbling down the side of the cup, and dumped the contents in the sink. She was *not* going back to hiding in the house, waiting for someone else to do something. Alison would or would not ever speak to her again. But whether she would or would not go back to being a fungus was up to her and no one else.

To the pulsing beat of Alannah Myles, she cleaned out the freezer and refrigerator, made a grocery list and then set off for the store. She'd read somewhere that it wasn't a good idea to shop on an empty stomach and a good old-fashioned American burger sounded like ambrosia — and not a fast-food burger either. She'd try the little place Alison had once taken her to. It was clear across town, but it would be about as far from sitting in front of the television eating plastic food as she could get. And the drive was lovely with everything green and the last of the spring flowers in bloom. The thought of Alison was accompanied by a pang, but the chances of running into Alison were slim. Now that she thought about it, Alison was rarely in her office on Thursday afternoons so she was safe. She sang as she drove and could picture Nick covering her ears. Ah, Nick. It was good to be home, but she was already starting to miss Nick's face, and eyes and hands and ... well, everything else. Had she been incredibly stupid to walk away from that magic?

Since the lunch crowd had left, she found a table facing the patio off the street. She waited for her meal in the cool shade of the red-and-white striped umbrella. Sunlight tickled her arms as it filtered through the scarlet blooms of the oleander bush behind her. Midtown was on a different time schedule, she decided. The cars appeared to not be going the speed limit. People didn't walk, they strolled. Across H Street she could see shoppers casually examining the window of a toy store. Other diners were reading newspapers. The waiter stopped to chat when he delivered her salad and burger — nothing to say really, just how nice the weather was. Carolyn thought she could have been in a Parisian café, enjoying life, but everything around her was familiar. It was home.

"Hi, stranger. Your tan says you've been somewhere very sunny."

Carolyn jumped. Not Alison, but Alison's assistant. "Hi, Devon. How are you?" She suddenly realized she was scared to death at the idea of seeing Alison. She'd written to Alison that she felt the same way as she always had about her. That was true as far as it went, but she hadn't understood what those feelings were. She couldn't let Alison discover them, either.

"Overworked as always — I'm ordering take-out. I'm slaving as usual while the boss gallivants around a baseball field." He hesitated, looking as if he'd like to join her, but also as if he thought it might not be a good idea.

"Please," Carolyn said, "have something to drink while you wait. I recommend slow sipping, feeling the sun on your face and appreciating the breeze."

Devon sat down opposite her and ordered a tall lemonade from the waiter who appeared from nowhere. The two men discussed just what a tall lemonade meant and Carolyn realized, in mid-swallow, that they were flirting. She choked and then was glad of an excuse for her rapidly reddening face. Devon was gay ... so how could Alison have reacted the way she had? Maybe she didn't know about Devon.

Carolyn studied Devon when he wasn't looking. As they talked, she realized that if she'd had "lesbian eyes" in the past she'd have seen that Devon was gay. She'd always thought him good-looking, with smooth black skin and enigmatic eyes. It wasn't his gray slacks and white shirt, or the red and navy blue tie loosened at his collar. Just something ... different, something more open, stronger and yet gentler than what she thought of as typically male. *And what do I know about typical males?* Absolutely nothing, she told herself. It was clear from his choice of non-work-related topics that he knew something was wrong between Alison and Carolyn — he hadn't hesitated to talk about work in the past.

He had finished his lemonade, his takeout was bagged and ready, before Carolyn found the courage to blurt out, "How is she?"

"She's fine." Devon tensed as if he would stand up, then remained in his chair. "She's okay. I, uh, gathered the surprise didn't go over too well."

"She was the one who was surprised," Carolyn said slowly. "If ... if you wanted to try to mend fences with her, how would you go about it?"

Devon looked at her for a minute, then one side of his mouth quirked slightly. "Make her mend her half, to begin with. I know you had some sort of disagreement, but I don't think I'm telling tales if I say she's miserable about it. She might not know you want to talk."

"But I wrote ..." Carolyn let her voice trail away. "It's not your problem, but thank you."

"My pleasure. Well, I have to get back. Next time I see you maybe you'll have another Carly Vincent sizzler under one arm."

"Don't count on it," Carolyn said. "Carly has lost touch with her audience ... so to speak." She was pretty sure Devon was gay, but how did she let him know they now had something in common. A secret hand signal?

Devon smiled. "She's too irresponsible not to get back in touch. See you 'round."

She watched him leave and grinned when she saw the waiter watching him too. His belief in Carly Vincent's tenacity was very kind, but Carolyn had no intention of getting back in touch with the old audience for her romances. Carly Vincent had contracted a condition fatal to heterosexual romance and Carolyn Vincense really needed to think about her future.

But what about getting in touch with a new audience? She froze in mid-chew. Now *that* was an idea worth pursuing. It would take some research, but she'd always been good at that. By the time she'd finished lunch and bought her groceries she couldn't wait to get started.

She dove into her research with an intensity she'd never felt in college — this research was about herself. She found the women's and gay bookstores, made some extensive acquisitions, and then bought copies of the trade magazines that dealt with books for gay and lesbian readers. She studied them as she had studied similar publications dealing with romances and mainstream publishing. She noted themes, controversies and critical focus. She began typing notes into her computer and laughed at herself when she titled the document "Lesbian 101." After a while she found she had to divide the document into pieces: sex, politics, living arrangements, the law, family relationships, children, coming out, history ... the project grew bigger and bigger. As an ex-English major, she most enjoyed the articles and books about women poets and authors of the past. Women's studies was an entire world she'd known existed, but had never personally explored. It was high time.

After two solid days she was daunted by what she did not know. It would be quite some time before she wrote anything reflecting her new view of herself and her world. She had successfully put Nick out of her mind and ignored the continued silence from Alison. Sometimes, though, in the middle of the night, her body would become molten with desire — images of Nick fanned the fire higher and higher. But when she closed her eyes it was Alison's dark hair and glistening body that intensified her passion. She found it hard to believe that only a few short months ago she had decided once and for all she was frigid. She wanted to see Alison, but dreaded it. She suspected her heart would confirm something she was sure Alison would reject, feelings that could jeopardize whatever friendship they could salvage.

Despite her absorption with her research, her appointment with Samantha Beckwith to discuss the completed work and expenditures was a welcome diversion. Now she knew why she felt flustered and tongue-tied when Samantha walked through the door — Samantha was gorgeous.

"You have to go from room to room and rhapsodize about everything I did," Samantha announced with a teasing smile. "I want r-a-v-e reviews."

"That'll be easy. There isn't anything I don't love." They wandered from the living room to dining room and spent a long time in the kitchen, contemplating a change of tile and countertop to avoid the expense of further renovations. When they moved to the bedroom, Carolyn was unreserved in her praise. "I love this room the most. I feel like a grown up, and the new bed is wonderful."

"That's gratifying. It was a real find," Samantha said. Carolyn thought Sam must be very pleased because she was absolutely blushing. Her dark cheeks were stained with red. They left the bedroom and Samantha hesitated at the door of Carolyn's office. "Have you given any thought to this room?"

"I don't think I want to change anything," Carolyn said. "I like the new area rugs." She led the way into the room, realizing too late that some of her new books — *Lesbian Love Advisor*, *Sex Variant Women in Literature* and *More Dykes To Watch Out For* — were stacked on the desk.

She saw Sam hesitate, then put her hand on the top book. "I love these cartoons, don't you?" Then she was examining all of the other books, mentioning the ones she'd read.

After a prolonged silence, Carolyn finally found her voice. "It's a new field of study," she said with a shaky laugh. "I . . . learned a lot while I was away."

"Welcome, then," Samantha said with a reassuring smile. Her smile faded. She looked puzzled and started to say something but shook her head. "So, umm, you don't want to do anything else in here?"

"Not yet," Carolyn said. "It's a work in progress."

Sam paused at the front door. "Would you like to come to a softball game, meet some women?"

Carolyn gasped, stared at her feet, then said with what she knew must be an idiotic smile, "Sure." She wrote down the date and time of the next game. "I'll be there. It sounds like fun."

When Sam left, Carolyn could have sworn she was muttering something about being a fool.

♥

Dinner with Curt, Margot and the boys was the usual contained uproar, but the boys settled into bed readily enough to listen to Carolyn's promised story. She made it a good one, spinning it out for a long time, and finished when her audience nodded off. She was only prolonging her own agony.

She shut the boys' door quietly and went downstairs and out to the patio where Margot and Curt would be enjoying the warm May evening. Memorial Day weekend promised to be a hot one, as always, with temperatures reaching the one hundred degree mark by the Monday holiday.

Carolyn paused at the screen door, giving Margot and Curt a few more moments alone as they sat quietly talking in the near dark. *I can do this*. She had not mentally prepared for any alternatives — she could only hope that the affection they always showed her was true. She took a deep breath, then stepped out on the patio. "You must live for this moment every day, when they're asleep."

"You can't imagine," Margot said. "I love them, but the best part of the day is still bedtime. Do you want some more coffee?"

"No, I'm fine."

There was silence, and before Curt or Margot could bring up another subject, Carolyn got up to turn on the patio light. She wanted to see their faces. Then she sat on the edge of her lounger and leaned toward them.

"I have to tell you the rest about Europe. The pictures don't say what happened to me."

"Margot was right," Curt said. "You look different. Pleased, but — dare I say it? You look older, too."

"It wasn't that long," Carolyn said, "but I do feel older. I had an affair. The most incredible, passionate affair imaginable. It opened new doors in me. It opened new worlds to me. I'll never be the same."

"But why aren't you ..." Margot's question faded away as Carolyn smiled ruefully.

"I'll get into why I'm no longer having an affair. What I want to concentrate on now ... what I have to tell you is ..." Carolyn stumbled for words. All the research and rehearsal in the world didn't make this easy. "Okay. I had an affair with another woman. I found out I'm a lesbian."

Curt was still. Margot's eyes went round as she stared at Carolyn.

"Nobody pushed me. I didn't do it because I hate men, or because I was curious or lonely. I found myself incredibly attracted to another woman and I acted on my feelings. Now I know why the marriage didn't work, why dating never felt right. And I've discovered a beautiful world of possibility that I can't wait to explore. I couldn't keep my discovery from you."

To Carolyn's dismay, tears trickled down Margot's face. "Margot, I'm sorry this has upset you —"

Margot waved a hand at her, interrupting. "No, no it isn't you. It's ... Curt, you tell her while I get a Kleenex." She hurried inside.

Curt looked stricken. "What do I say, Carrie? Congratulations?"

"No. But don't worry about me. Save your congratulations for when I find a nice woman and settle down." Cripes, she thought to herself — I still want the same thing I ever did. She wasn't sure if that was good or bad.

He smiled slightly. "You deserve the best, you know. I'll try not to worry — but you are my baby sister. Nothing's too good for you." His smile broadened. "And I'm proud of your courage. I'm glad you told me. I just don't know what to say." He ducked his head and muttered in an embarrassed brotherly fashion, "And I'll always love you. You should know that."

Carolyn gave a sigh of relief. He'd said everything she could possibly hope for. "But what upset Margot?"

Curt looked up again. "She got a letter from her aunt in Toronto a few weeks ago. A cousin of hers, her age, died of AIDS. Nobody in the family knew he was sick because he stayed away. He couldn't find the courage to tell them."

"Jerome was my first crush," Margot said from the patio doorway, a tissue box in hand. "He was so dashing and adult. I hadn't seen him in years, though." She sat down and Curt put his arm around her. "He died in a hospice in New York and my aunt can't forgive herself because she knows she discouraged honesty from him. If I'd kept up correspondence maybe he would have told me, or let me know he was sick — but I was just a little girl to him." Her eyes glittered with tears. "When I read the letter I thought to myself if either of my boys are gay I pray that I can make them trust me enough to tell me. I don't ever want to lose them to silence." She broke down again as the tears spilled over.

Carolyn sniffed and Curt's eyes were glittering. Carolyn reached for the tissue box. "I think I feel a group hug coming on."

When the tears stopped, Carolyn found herself telling them about Nick and why it wouldn't have worked. Margot told her she should get on the next plane back to London. Curt said she'd done the right thing.

"I can tell you two are going to be a big help with my love life," Carolyn said.

"I reserve the right to look over anyone you might be considering," Curt said. "Just like Dad would have."

"Do you think Mom and Dad —" Carolyn began. Curt was already nodding.

"Of course they would have," Margot said. "Look at the two great kids they raised. Now my folks, that's another story." Curt groaned in agreement and the conversation turned to in-laws and Carolyn found herself on the receiving end of lots of unsolicited advice about choosing a good mate.

When Carolyn got home she sat on the edge of her new bed and cried. She was pretty sure she was crying because she was happy. And maybe she was crying because the more she read, the more she realized how lucky she was to be gay and still have her family's love.

♥

Alison stood awkwardly a few feet back of second base, staring at Sam's back. Under other circumstances she and Sam would have been standing together at second base, watching the spectators, or pumping each other up for the game. They'd been buddies and Alison missed it. She didn't have so many friends that she could afford to lose one. She trudged to the pitcher's mound on the excuse of talking to the pitcher during her warm-ups, then walked toward second base, her steps slowing as she reached the spot where Sam graced the playing field.

"I miss being your friend," Alison said softly.

Sam smiled, a mixture of regret and resignation. "I miss you too. I'm sorry I messed it up by falling in love with you," she said in a low voice. "But hey,

I'm recovering. And I want you to remember that I'll be your friend for a lot longer than we were ever lovers. And I can prove it." Her expression lightened and there was an unmistakable twinkle in her eyes.

Why, Alison asked herself, why don't I love this woman back? "Okay, prove it." She met Alison's gaze for a moment, then lifted her chin in the direction of the smattering of onlookers in the stands along the third-base line. Alison turned, shading her eyes, trying to see what Sam meant.

The centerfielder joined them, saying, "New woman in the stands, guys. Top row, two from the left. Yowza, what legs."

Then Alison saw her — *her* — standing on the top row of the bleachers. She was digging in a satchel, triumphantly producing a pair of sunglasses. Alison knew she only had a few seconds before Carolyn started to study the players. So she stared. The jeans were cut tight and the legs much longer than Alison remembered. The fair skin glowed with a light tan. The bright white of a shirt was dazzling. A rose splashed across one breast and Alison hungrily absorbed the tantalizing strip of browned skin between the shirt and jeans. Alison wanted in the worst way to see it up close. The sun turned Carolyn's hair to gold, but the sunglasses made her expression mysterious. Alison realized then that Carolyn had seen her. To her amazement, Carolyn waved casually, then stared back, hands on hips that had never seemed so sexy.

"Hey, McNamara, stop drooling and get your butt into right field," the coach shouted. Alison blushed furiously and hurried to her position, hoping Carolyn hadn't heard.

Sam's voice followed her. "So am I your friend, or what?"

The way Alison saw it, she had limited options. She could concentrate on her game and ignore Carolyn. Fat hairy chance. Or she could go all out and try to make every catch look spectacular and have the game of her life, displaying all her machisma for the gal of her dreams. It was not something she could count on. Basically, she wanted only one thing — not to make a fool of herself.

She partially succeeded. She overthrew second base on an easy force out and got caught off first base trying to steal. It could happen to anyone, right? By the top of the ninth they were behind one run and Alison was pretty sure she'd made it through the game respectably. Sam had led off the bottom of the inning with a double and been advanced to third on a sacrifice fly, so now she represented the tying run. Then the batter before her grounded out, leaving her facing two outs. She'd represent the winning run if only somehow she made it around the bases.

As Alison stepped to the plate she decided she was getting payback for the mess she'd made of her love life. She was playing Mighty Casey in front of a former lover and the woman she loved, not to mention the women she knew who would razz her mercilessly if she struck out. It was early in the season and everybody — *everybody* — knew her hitting didn't get hot until August. But it was not August. The first pitch, a fast, sinking slider, whistled past Alison and slapped into the catcher's mitt before Alison even had a chance to get the bat off her shoulder. Strike one.

Okay, I'm in deep shit, she told herself. A curve, it'll be a curve. She guessed right, got a healthy piece of it and took off. She was headed for second and Sam was across home plate when the umpire called the ball foul. Damn. It had had the length to get over the fence, but had finally curved into the parking lot. The fans sat down again, their spiraling cheer of excitement fading into either groans of disappointment or sighs of relief.

Her heart was pounding from running and anxiety. She fouled off the next pitch — a piece of shit sucker ball. She stared at the pitcher and decided she was about to get a sizzler. She was right. She connected, but not solidly and knew the ball was going to fall somewhere in deep centerfield.

Alison lived by one rule of batting: if you hit it, run like hell. She ran. And when the centerfielder caught the fly ball she'd just keep running, right out of the park all the way home to hide in shame. The ball hung for a long time. As she rounded second she saw the centerfielder scrambling into position, her glove raised. The right fielder was streaking toward the same area to back up the catch. They were both calling for the ball. Sam was already at home plate, screaming and jumping. She headed for third and when the crowd collectively gasped and then started hollering she guessed the ball hadn't been caught. She didn't have the time to look back — she looked at the base coach. Shit, she was being waved home.

"Run!" Alison could hear from her teammates shouting from the dugout. As she passed the stands on the third base line, Alison could swear she heard one particular voice chanting, "Run, Alison, run!"

Sam screamed, "Slide inside!"

Alison hit the ground on her chest, her right arm extended. When she stopped sliding she looked up through the choking dust. She could feel the smooth plate under her palm. Ringing in her ears was the one word she wanted to hear, drawn out into two syllables by a hoarse umpire: "Seeeee-afe!"

The catcher threw her mitt and mask to the ground in disgust. Alison squealed when Sam jumped on her and within seconds everyone was playing dog-pile-on-Alison. Alison was laughing hysterically and thinking *God, I love this game.* Then her scraped chest started to send needles of pain through her body. Her leg felt like she'd pulled a muscle in her calf, probably as she rounded third. Her arm ached enough to be broken. She pushed at the bodies on her with more and more force.

"Get off, I'm dying. Get off!" Abruptly, the women moved aside. Alison looked up. Two of her teammates had a cooler full of Gatorade. Alison scrambled, but didn't get out of the way in time. She was drenched. Green liquid dripped into her eyes.

Sputtering, she got to her feet, shaking her jersey away from her soaked body. She wiped her eyes and looked right into Carolyn's concerned face. Oh fine, she thought, there's nothing like having no dignity at all.

"You're bleeding," Carolyn said.

Alison looked down her jersey. Red blotches were starting to mix with the green goo. She winced. "That stuff was not made to clean wounds."

"Hey, sorry, Al, didn't realize," said the woman with the empty cooler.

"It's okay. At least it's washed away some of the dirt."

"Everybody, this is Carolyn," Sam announced. "She's . . . new."

Someone quipped back, "Yeah, but is she single?"

Her color high, Carolyn said, "Do you need help getting home?"

Alison bent over, her hands on her thighs. "I'm okay."

"Sam'll take care of her," the coach said. Everyone laughed except Carolyn, Sam and Alison.

Carolyn looked quickly at Sam, who stared at her feet. She then studied Alison and Alison heard her say under her breath, "Oh . . ."

Alison looked up. "I'm going to be a mess tomorrow," she said to Carolyn. "But can I take you out to dinner? So I can . . . explain and apologize."

"You don't have to do that," Carolyn said. She bit her lower lip, making a red spot in an increasingly pale face.

"Yeah, I do." She took a step and limped. Yep, she'd pulled a muscle. She saw Carolyn start forward, but Sam was there first, steadying her.

"I'm already filthy," Sam said to Carolyn. "You don't want this v-i-l-e green stuff on your gorgeous shirt. It looks like a little something you picked up in Italy."

"It is," Carolyn said, her voice distracted.

"So we're on for dinner," Alison pressed Carolyn.

"Okay." Carolyn was staring at the ground.

"I'll pick you up at seven," Alison said.

"Okay." Carolyn studied Alison's jersey for a moment, then said, "Well, I guess I'll head home. It was a great game. See you later. 'Bye Sam. 'Bye everybody." She walked away, her brown feet clinging gracefully to espadrilles.

"Come on, slugger," Sam said, half-carrying the limping Alison toward the dugout. "And put your tongue back in your mouth before you bite it off. And one last thing, I want to be best maid at the wedding." Sam sighed when Alison let out an hysterical giggle.

♥

Carolyn dressed with care for dinner. She tried on at least four different outfits, discarding each one because Alison had seen it. She looked over the clothes she'd bought in Europe. The new black silk pantsuit was the obvious choice. She chose a thin shell in brilliant emerald to wear under the jacket and then studied herself critically. No, it was all wrong for Alison. Nick had said Carolyn looked edible in that combination, but Carolyn couldn't dress that way for Alison. Color flamed in her face as she remembered the outline of Alison's body under her drenched jersey.

Alison and Sam. It had come as a shock. Carolyn still couldn't control a shiver of dismay every time she thought of it. She did not understand why Alison had reacted the way she had in Rome, and her own feelings were entirely too complex — a double blow of realizing Alison was also a lesbian and that she was quite unavailable. Her heart had headed for the moon only to drop back into reality with a thud. She continued to reexamine their past friendship. Alison had never indicated ... anything, but then Carolyn hadn't been ready for anything.

She looked at herself in the mirror again. She saw what Nick had meant about edibility. She changed the shell to a less flattering yellow. There. She was ready for dinner and ready to scream.

The doorbell rang before she had the chance to consider changing again. Alison stood nervously in the foyer. Carolyn recognized her outfit in an instant — Alison had bought it at Carolyn's insistence. The vivid purple shirt bloused over sleek patterned pants that tapered to Alison's ankles. At the time, Carolyn had said it made Alison exotic, insisted Alison would turn heads. She'd been right — she'd just given herself whiplash.

"You know," Alison said, "it's a gorgeous day out there."

Carolyn laughed with relief, more at ease. She knew what Alison was getting at. "And you think it would be ideal if only we were in a convertible." Alison blinked innocently. "Okay, we'll take my car."

Alison helped her take the top off the Mustang and then Carolyn followed Alison's directions to drive them "Downtown, James, and step on it." At an intersection they were ogled by beer slime in a pickup and Carolyn understood, finally, why Alison had always been able to treat ogling men as if they could not be less important to her. She found herself giving them a look that was a twin sister's to

Alison's. After they pulled away she found herself grinning at Alison who laughed and hollered, "Yeeee-hah! It took you a while, but you finally saw the light!"

They weren't far from the women's bookstore in midtown when Alison told her to take any parking spot she found. Carolyn slammed on the brakes, backed up half a block and expertly parallel parked. "How's this?"

"Very nice," Alison said. "I need to see a chiropractor now, but otherwise, good. A nine point eight, taking into account the difficulty factor. With the Dixieland Jazz Festival in full swing, I thought we'd be looking for days."

"Do we have a reservation?" She hoped so — the restaurant up the street was packed with people, all of whom looked like they were from out of town. Heat radiated from the swell of bodies overflowing onto the sidewalk.

"Oh," Alison said, following Carolyn's gaze, "we're not going there. Around the corner and up a half a block."

They stopped at an unassuming doorway to a restaurant she had never noticed. It wasn't full and she noted that the diners were all women. They were shown to a table on the back patio.

"You never brought me here before," she said, regretting it immediately. What a stupid thing to say, she thought.

"Well, that was obviously a major mistake on my part. Let's order and then talk."

After they had selected entrees, there was an

awkward silence. She had felt much more comfortable in the car. The urge to scream became stronger.

"I'm sorry," Alison said suddenly. "I thought I had what I wanted to say all worked out."

"You don't have to say anything."

"Yeah I do. I've been gay since before I met you," Alison said. "I've always loved women. I kept waiting for a chance to tell you when we were rooming together, but it never came. And then I thought if I did tell you you wouldn't want to room together again. I liked you too much to risk it. And then it was too late. After five years, after ten, how could I just say, oh, by the way, there's something I meant to tell you ten years ago. It was easier not to talk about it, and we always had lots of other things to talk about."

"I understand." Carolyn sipped her water. "Really I do."

"And after college, when we stayed friends, I started to think I was in love with you. You were unattainable but that didn't matter. And then you got married and ..."

"You don't have to do this," Carolyn said, her heart beating high in her throat. She couldn't bring herself to meet Alison's gaze.

"I have to." Alison was quiet while their salads were served. "Anyway, when I decided to surprise you in Europe I was ready to tell you ... everything. And I was too late."

Alison wasn't the one who'd been too late — Carolyn had been too late to take the love offered. If only she'd seen it. She could feel hot color stealing into her cheeks. Perhaps it was for the best because it hadn't really been love. Just like what she'd felt for Nick hadn't really been love either. No, she wasn't in love. Not at all. "I'm sorry," she said.

"Don't be ... I acted like a spoiled child. I think I was more infatuated with the *idea* of being in love with you, but I'm over it. I've had time to reflect. I want to ... go back to the way we were. Best friends. I've missed you, for the last year," Alison said, her cheeks flushed. "I've missed you," she said again, softly.

"I've missed you, too." Carolyn looked down at her salad. "This looks good," she managed to say. Nuevo California cuisine — a single leaf of romaine was graced with two croutons and a lemon slice. She was hungry now. By the time she finished the salad she'd be starving.

They ate in silence. She noted for future reference that it only takes two minutes to eat a romaine lettuce leaf, no matter how small your bites are. Their plates were taken away and Alison, who had been carrying an unusually large purse, produced a wrapped package which she handed to Carolyn.

"What's this?"

"A coming out present."

Carolyn unwrapped it and found a publishing guide for gay and lesbian writers. "Is this a hint?" She gave Alison a suspicious smile.

"Oh yes. A very big hint," Alison said unashamedly. Her bravado softened as she said, "I just want you to know that nothing has to change between us."

We'll go on being all business, Carolyn thought. Well, it would do. She wanted their friendship back as well, but this was a start. "I've been thinking about it and — I'm glad we'll still be able to work together. If I do finally decide to start a book. I don't know. I don't really feel like a lesbian yet. I mean, I know I am, I told Curt ..."

"You told your brother?" Alison seemed amazed. "Just like that?"

"What else would I do?"

"What if he'd thrown you out?"

"Out of what? His life would have a hole in it if he didn't let me be a part of it. I'd live."

"Shit," Alison said. "Life is so easy for you."

"No, it's not." She felt slighted. "It was very hard."

"Don't you know why I never go home? I've been back twice in all the times I've known you. My mother invites men over for dinner while my father tells me all the things ACT UP has done and tells me to defend myself. Going home makes me miserable. So I don't."

"I'm sorry," Carolyn said. "But that doesn't make what I had to do any less difficult."

"Oh, I know," Alison said. "Your family is ... nice. There is no other word for it. Like politically correct Cleavers."

"I think I'm insulted."

"Don't be. I'm so jealous I could spit," Alison said. "Oh, I almost forgot this." She handed Carolyn a newspaper clipping. "Devon saw this in the *New York Times*."

226

Carolyn saw Nick's picture. "You told Devon about Nick?"

"Actually, all I told Devon was that there was a hell of a book in Nicolas Frost's future — we were brainstorming new business. Music industry people — go ahead and read it — are already speculating that the Maestro's soon-to-be-released first recording has Grammy potential."

Carolyn skimmed the article. "I have to start a scrapbook," she said absently. "This is a very flattering piece. She really is arriving." She told herself she'd done the right thing. Given up incredible passion with Nick so she could come home and *not* be in love with Alison. Right. She glanced at Alison and an awkward silence fell between them, dispelled by the fortuitous arrival of their entrees.

"Yummy," Carolyn said. Her shrimp in garlic sauce was really cream sauce with two butterflied shrimp, three brussels sprouts and a baby carrot. It did look gorgeous on the plate. Her stomach growled. She realized Alison was laughing.

"I come here because it's woman-owned and organic," Alison said. "And when I'm dieting. Eat hearty."

Carolyn tried to eat slowly and savor the subtle flavors, but it only took a few minutes to nibble up the shrimp. She even gagged down the brussels sprouts. When their server offered to bring a dessert menu, Carolyn refused, saying she couldn't possibly manage another bite. Alison paid the check, the epitome of elegance, and then they walked slowly back to the car.

As she buckled up, Carolyn's stomach growled — loudly. Alison dropped her *hauteur* and said, "I'm starving too. So much for elegance. Let's go to a drive-thru."

Carolyn didn't need another hint. The Mustang achieved G-force when it leapt out of the parking space.

11

Harmonics

Within a mere five minutes they had left midtown and were crossing the American River. Carolyn swooped down Fair Oaks Boulevard, headed for fast-food row. "Where do you want to go?"

"How about the Colonel?"

"You got it." She swore as a car cut her off, making her slow down and subsequently miss the longest light in Sacramento County. As they coasted to a stop, she ran her fingers through her hair. Any semblance of style had been ruined by the wind. "This is just like old times."

"No, it's not."

Alison's tone was so serious that Carolyn looked at her in surprise. Alison was pale underneath her healthy tan. "What's wrong?"

"It's not like old times." She was shaking her head. "Oh shit. I thought I could do this."

"Do what?"

"Be friends." There was a trace of a smile on Alison's face. Her eyes were huge and Carolyn found herself getting lost in them.

"Don't say that," Carolyn whispered. "Why can't we go on being friends? Ally, don't ruin it."

"I can't help it." Alison was staring dully ahead of her, then she suddenly slammed her fist on the dash. "God damn it, how can I possibly be friends with you," she shouted, "when I'm in love with you!"

Carolyn's foot slipped off the clutch. The car jumped, then stalled. She got the Mustang started and then said, as casually as she could manage, "What about Sam?"

"Sam's history. I've been in love with you for *ages*."

Carolyn looked around. The corner of Fair Oaks Boulevard and Howe Avenue. Henceforth a sacred site. Her lips curved in a faint smile that grew. "Yeeee-hah," she said quietly to Alison.

"What about Nick?" Alison's dazed expression hadn't changed.

Carolyn stared past Alison at the middle-aged man and woman who were listening to their entire conversation from the safety of their Fairmount. She grinned at the woman and inclined her head at Alison. "She's in love with me."

"But what about Nick," the woman asked, dead serious.

Carolyn fought back a bubble of laughter. "Nick's history."

"Oh good," the woman said. The light turned green. The man at the wheel of the Fairmount gave Carolyn a wild-eyed look and floored it. The Mustang pulled out more sedately.

Carolyn turned into the drive-thru lane of the Kentucky Fried Chicken. She turned to Alison. "What would you like, darling?"

Alison blinked at her. "Just like that? I say I love you and you start calling me darling? It was that easy?" Alison shook her head. "That's all I ever had to do? Don't you realize what it means?"

"It means I'm permanently entitled to half your Sara Lee cheesecake forever."

"You sure do make a woman wait," Alison said slowly. "I've been wanting to kiss you for ages. Maybe from the first moment I saw you."

"Sweet talker," Carolyn said. There was no moonlight or roses, no candlelight or violins. Just the smell of fast food and the drone of traffic. Ah, bliss.

"*Are you ready to order?*" The speaker finally came to life.

Carolyn opened her mouth to give their usual order when she felt Alison's hands on her shirt. She squawked.

"*What was that,*" an impatient voice demanded from the speaker.

"A shake," Carolyn said. Alison's hands were

followed by her mouth. "Stop that.. Ally, not with the top down."

"We don't make shakes."

"Sorry. Uh, I want a nine-piece bucket."

"What kind of pieces?"

Alison's lips captured one nipple through the fabric of Carolyn's clothing. "Breasts."

"All breasts?"

"Yes, oh yes," Carolyn groaned. Alison's hand was at the seam where Carolyn's slacks met between her legs. "Okay, some thighs and legs, too."

"Mashed potatoes and gravy?"

Alison's head dropped to where her hand was pressing into Carolyn. Her teeth nibbled at the seam.

"Both," Carolyn gasped.

"Cole slaw?"

Carolyn held Alison's head against her body. Her legs were opening involuntarily and her foot was threatening to slip off the brake. "Oh yes." She took the car out of drive. "You have to stop. I'm going to lose total control. Someone is going to see us."

"What? Did you want something else?"

"I want to go down on you so badly," Alison said with a groaning gasp.

"Come again?"

"Oh God," Carolyn moaned. "Uh, that's all."

"Drive forward," the voice snapped.

"Alison, I have to drive the car," Carolyn said. She could hardly make her legs obey her.

Alison retreated to the other side of the car. Her smile was part self-confident seductress and part child who had just blown out all the candles on her birthday cake. "I have so many fantasies." She looked Carolyn up and down. "In another one you're not wearing pants."

Carolyn shivered and misaligned the car with the drive-thru window, something she had never done before. She backed up, missed again because her foot slipped on the brake, and then inched forward until she could see the woman behind the window. She took the red-and-white striped containers and passed them to Alison, handed over the money and drove away as quickly as she could. She had the sneaking suspicion the drive-thru clerk had seen Alison's antics. Oh well — it was hardly illegal. Her stomach growled again as the aroma of food hit her. She glanced at Alison ... she was simultaneously hungry for two very different things. "Why does stuff so bad for me smell so good? I'm starved."

"Here," Alison said. She broke off a hunk of biscuit and pushed it into Carolyn's mouth. "Eat as much of this as you can."

"What are you ... doing," Carolyn said between swallows.

"I don't intend to give you any time to eat food when we get home so this will have to do. I need to build up your strength." She took a bite out of a chicken leg then held it in front of Carolyn's mouth. "Bite."

By the time they pulled into her garage, she was partially sated. The food part. Alison pushed the button on the garage door remote and the door closed.

"Why did you do that? Now I can't see a thing," Carolyn said.

"Who cares?" Cardboard crunched and bags crumpled as Alison lunged across the bucket seats toward Carolyn.

Their bodies collided, their lips collided. Their breasts — and with a complete disregard for comfort — hips and crotches collided. Carolyn didn't know which way was up. She didn't care. Alison straddled her, managed to find the seat release and suddenly the seat plummeted backward. She fell back and Alison fell on top of her. Now they were getting somewhere.

"I've been wanting to make out with you in this car since college. Since college, do you hear me?" Alison, busy with Carolyn's shirt buttons, paused.

"I hear you. Don't stop. Talk and unbutton at the same time."

Alison giggled. At the first touch of her fingers on Carolyn's bare skin she gasped. Her voice was soft and uncertain. "I've wanted to touch you like this for such a long, long time."

Carolyn's laughter, fueled by the ringing joy she felt, died in her throat. She pulled Alison down to her and their bodies collided more gently this time, leaving Carolyn weak with heat and want. She couldn't help but compare the softness of Alison's lips to Nick's. Alison moaned and Carolyn had a sudden sense of vertigo. She clung to Alison as Alison spread her body over Carolyn. She did not think of Nick again.

Soft sweetness searched her mouth. Hands stroked her cheeks, her hair. Lips moved to her chin, her throat, her shoulders, then captured her bare breast; it ached in the sudden warmth and tenderness of Alison's mouth.

She ached to touch Alison, too, to give Alison every pleasure imaginable, to show Alison that she loved her. But her fingers fumbled with the tiny pearl buttons that went down the back of Alison's shirt. They'd be here all night.

"Bad choice on my part," Alison said. She sat upright and reached over her head. There was the sound of rending fabric and buttons bouncing onto the dashboard and against the steering wheel. "We'll be finding buttons for years."

"Umm-hmm," was all Carolyn could manage. She pulled Alison down to her again, shuddering as her arms filled with the weight of Alison's body. She could feel Alison's leg between hers. She explored Alison's back with her hands. "Don't you think we should go inside?"

"Probably." Alison's lips nibbled at Carolyn's chin. Then her throat.

"Kiss me," Carolyn whispered. "Please."

As their lips met the horn went off.

"Sorry," Alison said. "Maybe we should move inside."

"We could just move into the back seat. It'll be just like we were in college and hadn't wasted all these years."

"Oh my," Alison said. "Are you going to make all my fantasies come true? And will we still be friends?"

"Besty friends," Carolyn said. "So move on back here, besty friend."

They scrambled to the back, losing the rest of their clothing as they went. When Alison stretched out again over her, Carolyn shuddered at the shocking delight of Alison's naked body. "Is this happening?"

"Yes," Alison whispered in her ear. "And now I'm going to make love to you until you faint."

"No more joking," Carolyn said. She was aching in new places, in new ways.

"I'm not joking," Alison said. Her intensity caused a wave of goose pimples to break out all over Carolyn's body. Alison's mouth, warm and electric, found Carolyn's chin, then her throat, then her shoulders.

Carolyn went rigid at the warmth of Alison's breath whispering across her aching breasts — then moist softness, a soft touch of tongue, divine and sweet. She shut her eyes as the rest of her opened — she had no choice. She couldn't stop herself from showing how much she wanted and how little she could hold back.

Suddenly Alison stretched away from her. The car door opened and the dash board light illuminated them. Alison was so beautiful, so incredibly sensuous.

"I want to see you," Alison said. Her mouth returned to Carolyn's breasts, teasing the ache, making it worse, then soothing, pleasing, teasing again.

Carolyn ground her hips against Alison. "I knew, I knew you would touch me like this. I knew you would know." Carolyn opened her eyes only to lose herself in the depths of Alison's obsidian gaze. Alison never blinked as her hand moved slowly between

Carolyn's inviting legs. The depth of her emotion was betrayed by an indrawn gasp, by her teeth catching her lower lip as Carolyn stiffened, driving herself toward Alison's possessing fingers. Alison's eyes shone with fierce pleasure.

Carolyn gave way to the magic that carried her away yet held her fast against Alison's heaving body.

They finally went inside, but made it no farther than the hallway. Carolyn stumbled, Alison grabbed her and they fell in delightful unison, Alison on the bottom. Alison's mouth had never seemed so full. It begged to be kissed, softly and then more intensely. Finally, Alison broke away from Carolyn's demanding mouth and placed her hands on her shoulders. "Please," she said in a soft, needing voice Carolyn had never thought she would hear. Alison the competent, the strong, the incredibly powerful — Alison needed her. A flash of something almost spiritual left Carolyn exalted, and she kissed the softness of Alison's thighs.

Nectar and honey on her chin. Such succulence, to enjoy it so, to feel so joined, intimate, with passion and ecstasy filling her mouth. Alison was holding her head, her voice calling, urging. Carolyn drank her deeply, making quiet noises at the back of her throat, not whimpers, not moans, but quiet sounds that said yes and oh and wonderful and I'm coming, so quietly that only another making those sounds can hear. Sounds only for Alison, touches only for Alison, music only for Alison.

Once was not enough for anything. Twice was not enough either.

Alison cradled the exhausted Carolyn in her arms. She smiled. "Let's move to the bed," she said.

Carolyn groaned. "Alison, the chicken's getting cold."

Alison let a laugh of sheer joy bubble out of her. "It was stone cold an hour ago. I kicked over the gravy anyway." She swallowed, not believing her every dream had come true.

Alison let Carolyn sleep when they finally reached the bed. She watched Carolyn's face fall into innocent, peaceful lines and resisted the urge to kiss the corner of Carolyn's adorable mouth. Eventually she slept too, knowing she had to go to sleep in order to wake up next to Carolyn. Then she would be able to cross one more fantasy off the list. Considering how long she had fantasized about being with Carolyn it was probably going to take fifty years before all of them were realized. Alison was looking forward to every moment.

Epilogue

The interviewer looked seriously into the camera, her trademark lisp giving a brief background of her next guest.

"Are you sure the tape's going?" Alison said.

Carolyn hushed her insistently. "Yes. I'm trying to listen."

"*. . . announcement set the classical world on its collective ear. Tonight you'll meet the conductor everyone is talking about and hear in her own words*

why she chose the intermission of a performance with
the New York Philharmonic to make her
transformation from Nicolas to Nicola.'' The
interviewer turned from the camera, which panned
back to bring the other occupant of the set into
view.

"It's her!" Carolyn's squeal hit high C. "God, she
looks good."

"No lusting after old flames," Alison warned in a
humoring tone.

"I chose the time and place quite precisely," Nick
was saying. Carolyn thought she sounded more like
Oscar than ever. "I'd just collected my third
American Grammy in as many years; several
recording opportunities and a tour were scheduled.
The concert was being taped for public television and
New York has always been kind to me. The
opportunity presented itself."

"Let's roll that tape. Where are we in terms of the
symphony?"

"At the final chorus," Nick said. "The words here
are, 'Joyous as a knight victorious, love toward
countless millions swelling.' As a friend of mine once
quite succinctly summed it up, it makes the top of
your head come off."

Carolyn turned up the volume as the music
swelled through the TV speakers. "Oh my God," she
whispered. "She conducted without her score." Alison
was quiet, but her hand slipped over Carolyn's. Nick
was strained to the tips of her toes, her expressive
arms gathering up the music, channeling it and
letting it fly away. The tip of her baton was a blur.
The voices were crescendoing; Carolyn gripped

240

Alison's hand to the last note. When Nick's arms finally dropped to her sides she swayed. The musicians seemed exhausted. The applause gained momentum, as if the audience was not sure what they were seeing. It swelled when Nick turned and took her first bow.

"Okay," Alison said. "I'll go to any of her concerts with you."

Carolyn smiled at Alison. "You might even enjoy it."

The interviewer's face reappeared on the screen, her expression one of concern and sympathy. *"There's been backlash, hasn't there?"*

"As a matter of fact, the Royal Academy tried to withdraw its invitation for me to become a Fellow. I was asked, in a roundabout way, to be a good chap and not make any embarrassing scenes about it. It has nothing to do with my being a woman, you see, it's just that I'm ... notorious I think the word was."

"You've obviously decided not to be a good chap."

"Quite. Men of conscience all over the classical music world have called the Academy's attempt an outrage. In several cases, they've successfully applied pressure to the recording companies who tried to break their contracts with me. I've resigned myself to being the equivalent of the pink dye dentists use to show where you've missed the plaque." Nick's laugh was easy and relaxed.

"Has it been all bad?"

"Oh no, some truly wonderful things have happened. My contemporary male colleagues standing by me, for example. I've also heard of two directorships at major symphonies going to women for the first time in the respective symphonies' histories. I'd *like* to think I've contributed to these steps forward for women in music. Music itself is enriched every time women of talent are allowed to display it. On a lighter note, I've apparently started quite a rage in female concert wear. In some of the less stodgy orchestras some women have abandoned their traditional black gowns for tuxedos similar to what the men wear. That's very flattering."

The interview progressed as Nick explained the whys and wherefores of her first decision to pose as a man. Toward the end of the interview she described what went through her mind as she strode to the podium at a concert the week before, her hair ruffled slightly, her sleeves rolled back and hands ungloved.

"I could tell the musicians were dumbfounded. Several kept rubbing their eyes. After all, the change was very subtle. A murmur from the audience started. When we paused between movements of the symphony — Beethoven's *Ninth* is another reason I chose that night — I could hear the buzz. I don't suppose the audience was sure until I took my curtain call. But no one could deny the power of the *Ode to Joy,* so nobody stormed out or refused to applaud." Nick's smile could have set off fireworks.

"And what about the private life of Nicola Frost? How will that change?"

"That depends on other people, doesn't it? There's been considerable debate about my personal life and commentary about how I portrayed myself as a Don Juan, if you will, as a part of my cover as a man. I felt it was necessary, but I don't think anyone got hurt."

"None of the women you dated suspected you were a woman?"

"I never let anyone close to me, physically or emotionally. I'm hoping my isolation might be ending now that I'm not hiding my gender anymore."

"The situation seems to beg an obvious question about your sexuality. In the last week, for example, your constant escort has been another woman — the British writer Patricia Morgan."

Nick's smile grew more serious as her eyes narrowed. "I would think the answer is obvious."

"Are you saying you're a lesbian?"

"Yes I am."

"Would you like to say anything further on the topic?"

"Well, I suppose now that I've cleared that up, we'll *really* find out who puts music first."

Carolyn thought she could hear a psychic cheer that stretched from San Francisco to New York, from Key West to Seattle and all points in between . . . a cheer that then went around the world.

Later, after stopping several times in her writing to watch Alison as she slept, Carolyn finished her letter to Nick.

And so, all in all, you were splendid. I taped every second, even the commercials and the announcements beforehand.

She paused as Alison emitted a unique-to-Alison

snore. After three years and then some, Carolyn had thought she would have stopped thinking every little thing about Alison was marvelous, but she hadn't.

Of course if you keep up this fame and fortune stuff you may get knighted. Would they call you Sir or Dame? I somehow can't picture anyone calling you Dame. Insist on Sir Nicola Frost. You could be the first female Sir in centuries — there were a few way back when. Maybe you were one of them in a previous life, who knows?

Well, this is long enough and I've no more to say. Look for my next book in the fall. Alison predicts it'll top the lesbian bestseller list like the last one. I hope you soon find someone to make delicious moans on the midnight hour with. I recommend it. Meanwhile, keep safe and happy. All my love as always and a little bit of Alison's as usual,

Carolyn

She dropped her tablet and pen by the bedside and turned out the light. Alison murmured in her sleep as Carolyn settled down beside her.

"What time is it?" Alison's voice was childlike in its drowsiness.

"Too late for you to worry about it," Carolyn said. "Go back to sleep."

Under the covers Alison's hand slowly meandered from Carolyn's stomach to one breast, then a finger lightly traced Carolyn's lips. "What if I don't want to?"

Carolyn inhaled the scent of what they had done before Alison had fallen asleep. "If you want to start again I'm going to need something for energy."

"Drive-thru? We could go to our special Kentucky

Fried." Alison's voice was a lot less sleepy. Her finger paused in its tracing of Carolyn's chin.

Carolyn nibbled Alison's finger. Her arms and legs turned to liquid at the thought of Alison's familiar passion that was always somehow new. "Not tonight. I have everything I could possibly want right here."

Alison laughed. "Does that mean I'm finger lickin' —"

Carolyn smothered the last word with a kiss that said yes.

About the Author

Karin's first crush on a woman was the local librarian. Just remembering the pencil through the loose, attractive bun makes her warm. Maybe it was the librarian's influence, but for whatever reason, at the age of 16 Karin fell into the arms of her first and only sweetheart.

There's a certain symmetry to the fact that ten years later, after seeing the film *Desert Hearts*, her sweetheart descended on the Berkeley Public Library to find some of "those" books. The books found there were the encouragement Karin needed to forget the so-called "mainstream" and spin her first romance for lesbians. That manuscript became her first novel, *In Every Port*.

The happily-ever-after couple now lives in the San Francisco Bay area, and became Mom and Moogie to Kelson in 1995 and Eleanor in 1997. They celebrate their twenty-eighth anniversary in 2005.

All of Karin's work can now be found at Bella Books. Details and background about her novels, and her other pen name, Laura Adams, can be found at www.kallmaker.com.

Publications from
BELLA BOOKS, INC.
The best in contemporary lesbian fiction

P.O. Box 10543, Tallahassee, FL 32302
Phone: 800-729-4992
www.bellabooks.com

DREAM LOVER by Lyn Denison. 188 pp. A soft, sensuous, romantic fantasy.
ISBN 1-931513-96-1 $12.95

NEVER SAY NEVER by Linda Hill. 224 pp. A classic love story . . . where rules aren't the only things broken.
ISBN 1-931513-67-8 $12.95

PAINTED MOON by Karin Kallmaker. 214 pp. Stranded together in a snowbound cabin, Jackie and Leah's lives will never be the same.
ISBN 1-931513-53-8 $12.95

WIZARD OF ISIS by Jean Stewart. 240 pp. Fifth in the exciting Isis series.
ISBN 1-931513-71-4 $12.95

WOMAN IN THE MIRROR by Jackie Calhoun. 216 pp. Josey learns to love again, while her niece is learning to love women for the first time.
ISBN 1-931513-78-3 $12.95

SUBSTITUTE FOR LOVE by Karin Kallmaker. 200 pp. When Holly and Reyna meet the combination adds up to pure passion. But what about tomorrow?
ISBN 1-931513-62-7 $12.95

GULF BREEZE by Gerri Hill. 288 pp. Could Carly really be the woman Pat has always been searching for?
ISBN 1-931513-97-X $12.95

THE TOMSTOWN INCIDENT by Penny Hayes. 184 pp. Caught between two worlds, Eloise must make a decision that will change her life forever.
ISBN 1-931513-56-2 $12.95

MAKING UP FOR LOST TIME by Karin Kallmaker. 240 pp. Discover delicious recipes for romance by the undisputed mistress.
ISBN 1-931513-61-9 $12.95

THE WAY LIFE SHOULD BE by Diana Tremain Braund. 173 pp. With which woman will Jennifer find the true meaning of love?
ISBN 1-931513-66-X $12.95

BACK TO BASICS: A BUTCH/FEMME ANTHOLOGY edited by Therese Szymanski—from Bella After Dark. 324 pp.
ISBN 1-931513-35-X $14.95

SURVIVAL OF LOVE by Frankie J. Jones. 236 pp. What will Jody do when she falls in love with her best friend's daughter?
ISBN 1-931513-55-4 $12.95

LESSONS IN MURDER by Claire McNab. 184 pp. 1st Detective Inspector Carol Ashton Mystery.
ISBN 1-931513-65-1 $12.95

DEATH BY DEATH by Claire McNab. 167 pp. 5th Denise Cleever Thriller.
ISBN 1-931513-34-1 $12.95

CAUGHT IN THE NET by Jessica Thomas. 188 pp. A wickedly observant story of mystery, danger, and love in Provincetown.
ISBN 1-931513-54-6 $12.95

DREAMS FOUND by Lyn Denison. Australian Riley embarks on a journey to meet her birth mother . . . and gains not just a family, but the love of her life.
ISBN 1-931513-58-9 $12.95

A MOMENT'S INDISCRETION by Peggy J. Herring. 154 pp. Jackie is torn between her better judgment and the overwhelming attraction she feels for Valerie.
ISBN 1-931513-59-7 $12.95

IN EVERY PORT by Karin Kallmaker. 224 pp. Jessica has a woman in every port. Will meeting Cat change all that?
ISBN 1-931513-36-8 $12.95

TOUCHWOOD by Karin Kallmaker. 240 pp. Rayann loves Louisa. Louisa loves Rayann. Can the decades between their ages keep them apart?
ISBN 1-931513-37-6 $12.95

WATERMARK by Karin Kallmaker. 248 pp. Teresa wants a future with a woman whose heart has been frozen by loss. Sequel to *Touchwood*.
ISBN 1-931513-38-4 $12.95

EMBRACE IN MOTION by Karin Kallmaker. 240 pp. Has Sarah found lust or love?
ISBN 1-931513-39-2 $12.95

ONE DEGREE OF SEPARATION by Karin Kallmaker. 232 pp. Sizzling small town romance between Marian, the town librarian, and the new girl from the big city.
ISBN 1-931513-30-9 $12.95

CRY HAVOC A Detective Franco Mystery by Baxter Clare. 240 pp. A dead hustler with a headless rooster in his lap sends Lt. L.A. Franco headfirst against Mother Love.
ISBN 1-931513931-7 $12.95

DISTANT THUNDER by Peggy J. Herring. 294 pp. Bankrobbing drifter Cordy awakens strange new feelings in Leo in this romantic tale set in the Old West.
ISBN 1-931513-28-7 $12.95

COP OUT by Claire McNab. 216 pp. 4th Detective Inspector Carol Ashton Mystery.
ISBN 1-931513-29-5 $12.95

BLOOD LINK by Claire McNab. 159 pp. 15th Detective Inspector Carol Ashton Mystery. Is Carol unwittingly playing into a deadly plan? ISBN 1-931513-27-9 $12.95

TALK OF THE TOWN by Saxon Bennett. 239 pp. With enough beer, barbecue and B.S., anything is possible! ISBN 1-931513-18-X $12.95

MAYBE NEXT TIME by Karin Kallmaker. 256 pp. Sabrina has everything she ever wanted—except Jorie. ISBN 1-931513-26-0 $12.95

WHEN GOOD GIRLS GO BAD: A Motor City Thriller by Therese Szymanski. 230 pp. Brett, Randi, and Allie join forces to stop a serial killer. ISBN 1-931513-11-2 $12.95

A DAY TOO LONG: A Helen Black Mystery by Pat Welch. 328 pp. This time Helen's fate is in her own hands. ISBN 1-931513-22-8 $12.95

THE RED LINE OF YARMALD by Diana Rivers. 256 pp. The Hadra's only hope lies in a magical red line . . . climactic sequel to *Clouds of War*. ISBN 1-931513-23-6 $12.95

OUTSIDE THE FLOCK by Jackie Calhoun. 224 pp. Jo embraces her new love and life.
ISBN 1-931513-13-9 $12.95

LEGACY OF LOVE by Marianne K. Martin. 224 pp. Read the whole Sage Bristo story.
ISBN 1-931513-15-5 $12.95

STREET RULES: A Detective Franco Mystery by Baxter Clare. 304 pp. Gritty, fast-paced mystery with compelling Detective L.A. Franco ISBN 1-931513-14-7 $12.95

RECOGNITION FACTOR: 4th Denise Cleever Thriller by Claire McNab. 176 pp. Denise Cleever tracks a notorious terrorist to America. ISBN 1-931513-24-4 $12.95

NORA AND LIZ by Nancy Garden. 296 pp. Lesbian romance by the author of *Annie on My Mind*. ISBN 1931513-20-1 $12.95

MIDAS TOUCH by Frankie J. Jones. 208 pp. Sandra had everything but love.
ISBN 1-931513-21-X $12.95

BEYOND ALL REASON by Peggy J. Herring. 240 pp. A romance hotter than Texas.
ISBN 1-9513-25-2 $12.95

ACCIDENTAL MURDER: 14th Detective Inspector Carol Ashton Mystery by Claire McNab. 208 pp. Carol Ashton tracks an elusive killer. ISBN 1-931513-16-3 $12.95

SEEDS OF FIRE: Tunnel of Light Trilogy, Book 2 by Karin Kallmaker writing as Laura Adams. 274 pp. In Autumn's dreams no one is who they seem. ISBN 1-931513-19-8 $12.95

DRIFTING AT THE BOTTOM OF THE WORLD by Auden Bailey. 288 pp. Beautifully written first novel set in Antarctica. ISBN 1-931513-17-1 $12.95